Gem
and the
Pegasus Crystal

Wendy A. Scott

To Bob

Enjoy this magical journey!

Crygem Publishing

Wendy A Scott.

Published in 2023 by Crygem Publishing

ISBN Paperback: 978-1-7393469-0-4
Ebook: 978-1-7393469-1-1

A CIP catalogue copy of this book can be found in the British Library.

Published with the help of Indie Authors World
www.indieauthorsworld.com

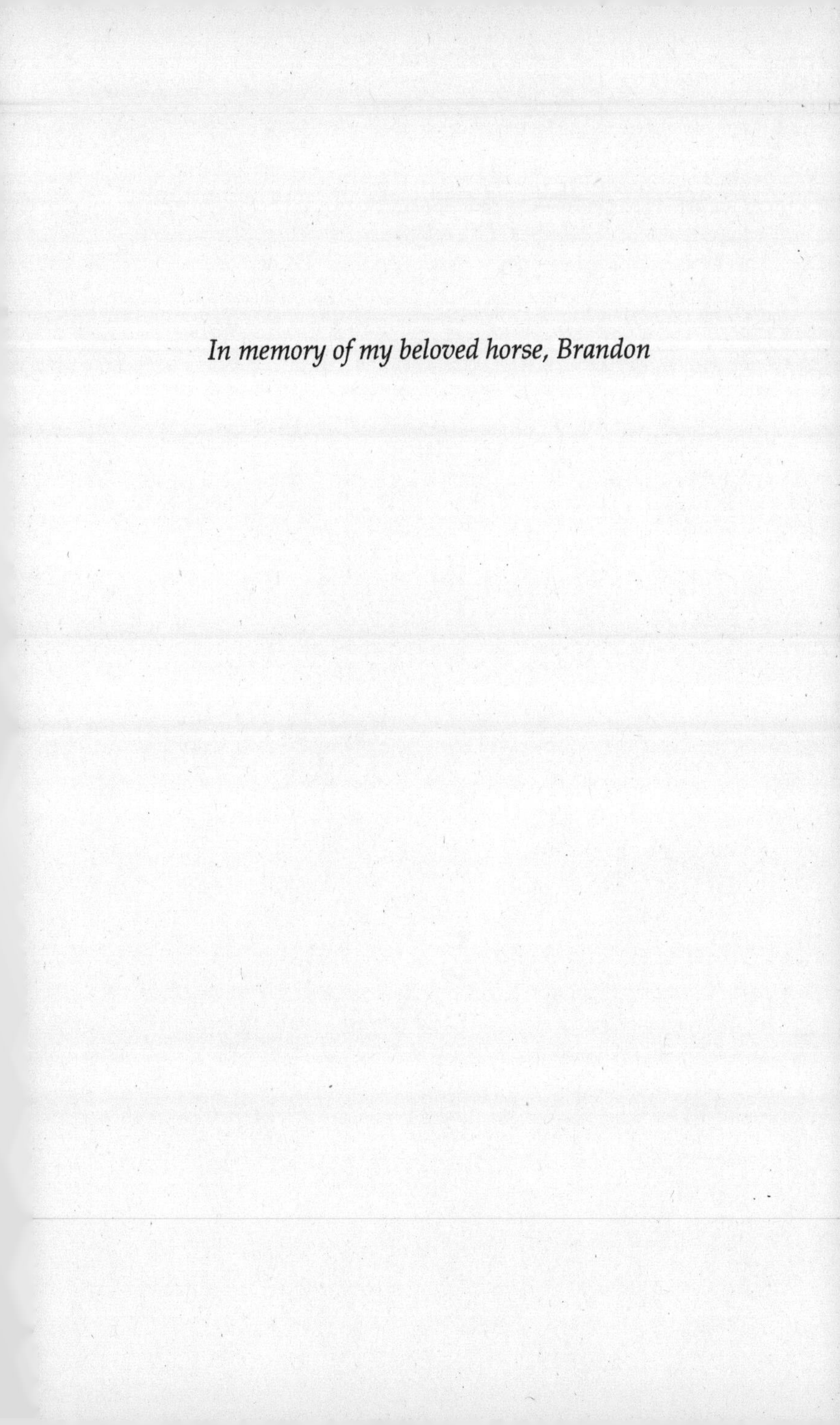

In memory of my beloved horse, Brandon

Acknowledgements

Thank you to William Stanfield — my partner and muse — for his creative, technological and editing skills; and my great friends Elaine Kennedy McIvor, Gordon Cassells, Gillian Downie, Christine Purdon, Gail Doyle and Dara Burns for their continued support and encouragement throughout my roller-coaster journey over the years researching, writing and editing this book.

To Kim and Sinclair MacLeod and Rachel Hessin, of Indie Authors World, who helped get me to the finishing post with their patience, professionalism and sense of humour!

My heartfelt thanks to you all for being there for me.

Special acknowledgements to the late G.W.S Barrow and his outstanding work - *Robert Bruce and the Community of the Realm of Scotland*

Introduction

The fictitious Arab state of Qamar is set between the existing (and very real) Arab Emirates of Dubai and Abu Dhabi, which are situated on the north east of the Arabian Peninsula where it meets the Persian Gulf.

Qamar's setting and characters obviously don't exist and are not based on any characters, real or previously created, except those actually in history. For the purposes of this novel Qamar is a modern, contemporary Arab state seeking to make its own way in a changing world.

Though the state has some oil interests, it has been struggling to modernize the country on behalf of the people while resisting western interest to expand its oil production. The capital city is Jaball and the state has a population of around 1.83 million people. Jaball is easily accessible to both Dubai and Abu Dhabi, via the interstate highway E11 which runs parallel to the coast.

Principally desert terrain, Qamar's access to the sea has ensured the country's importance in trading and fishing and is an important historical spice and silk trading hub.

It is against this background that the protagonists find themselves banded together to solve an ancient mystery and ensure all our futures.

PROLOGUE

Qamar, Middle East

The sound of automatic gunfire shattered the desert night air. As the beige and red microlight aircraft roared into the black night and up into the star-lit sky, Gemma looked up at the overhead, imposing sail-like structure constantly revealing the many colours of the rainbow; pink, lilac, orange and yellow, like a sunburst shooting up into the dark night.

It had been a close call but Prince Abdul and Gemma had escaped from the kidnappers' .camp and Gemma was looking forward to getting her feet back on terra firma and to the newspaper office at The Emirates Chronicle where she worked as a reporter.

Despite the warm, brown leather jacket Gemma was wearing, she felt a shiver run down her spine as the wind rummaged at her clothes like thousands of tiny hands and as she gazed around at the fearless desert, she felt relieved after the initial adrenaline rush high.

Crossing over the outskirts of Jaball, Abdul turned north again for the racecourse which he could see in the distance and through the microphones, said: "There it is; we'll start our descent soon. Tighten your restraints," he told Gemma.

No sooner had the words left his lips when they heard a loud crack and the microlight dropped suddenly and uncontrollably as one of the supporting struts of the right wing snapped.

Tumbling over and over like some grief-stricken prehistoric bird, they were thrown helplessly around accompanied by the scream of the engine. Parts of the wing tore off and were shredded by the propeller blades forcing the pair to instinctively crouch to avoid being hit.

Gemma grasped the sides of her chair like a motorcycle pillion passenger to counteract the g-forces. As the aircraft rapidly plunged downwards she was suddenly aware of the sound of silence.

Closing her eyes she screamed: "Abdul, help!" the colour draining from her tanned face. Prince Abdul had immediately carried out the emergency procedures and as Gemma struggled to comprehend what was happening, there was a sickening thud as the remains of the aircraft smacked off the corrugated roof of a building below, rolled, and then fell a further 20 feet to the ground.

As they finally came to rest the remains of the aircraft lay broken and shattered around them. Gemma tried to open her eyes but could not see. Her nose burned with the sharp smell of aviation fuel.

As she lay motionless on the hard ground, she could hear the faint sound of a horse whinnying in the distance.

Chapter One

Dubai Newsroom - Present Day

The soft yellow sun opened up gently against the azure-blue sky scattering glittering rays across the shimmering blue ocean below, bouncing off the iconic mirrored gigantic structure.

From the eighth floor of the Media City Building situated on Sheik Zayed Road, the huge floor-to-ceiling glass-windowed construction, known as Dubai Media City, Gemma had recalled with trepidation the first time she arrived in the newsroom and couldn't take in the vastness of all she surveyed from this height.

It was quite incredible and she still felt the feelings of vertigo looking down thousands of feet to the miniature city below reminding her of a toy town. The media building in Dubai was on the east side of the city and Gemma had been there a month since relocating from Scotland where she had cut her teeth in journalism working on local newspapers, magazines and dailies. Restless since the disappearance of her parents in South

America when she was very young, Gemma had been brought up by her grandmother in Edinburgh.

Lately, she had been agitated and her friend Sharon had suggested she tried International Journalism. It helped that Sharon worked in Dubai and had good contacts there. So, after a bit of arranging, Sharon managed to secure Gemma an interview which she sailed through. It was quite opportune that she had applied when she did, as the Emirates Chronicle, had just extended their offices to Jaball, a neighbouring city in the state of Qamar about fifty minutes' drive from Dubai. They needed extra staff at short notice.

Later, Gemma had tied up loose ends and said her goodbyes, hopped on a flight to the Arabic Emirate of Dubai and had arranged to lodge with Sharon until she could get an apartment of her own. But now she had been here a month and her friendship with Sharon had blossomed, looking for another place to stay was furthest from their minds.

Sharon had been a great help. A professional career woman herself, she had been a good friend, adviser, confidante and guide. The month had passed very quickly and Gemma had settled in quickly, though she resented being referred to as a 'cub reporter' as she had extensive journalistic experience back home. However, Gemma had persevered and had pitched a few good ideas at the morning editorial meetings.

As she watched the sunrise - in a hot desert country, work starts early and often runs late after a two hour midday break, during the hottest part of the day - her attention was drawn to a black speck travelling along the coast towards her location. Soon, she could feel the vibration of the rotors and saw the now familiar helicopter turn inland and head towards the media building.

The aircraft circled overhead and landed on the helipad located on the roof of her building. Gemma loved the hustle and bustle of a newsroom. No two days were the same. The newsroom took up the whole top floor. It was an open plan arrangement though journalists had a segregated area for each to work. Two offices were located in the corners of the building. One large office was split into staff rest rooms and toilets. The other was Wullie's 'lair'.

A pair of scarlet red shoes with seriously high skyscraper heels emerged from the passenger door of the helicopter followed by long, slim tanned legs, an on-the-knee straight cream skirt, matching silk blouse, and nipped-in waisted jacket. The woman was in her forties with poker-straight bobbed black hair, with a curious widow's peak parting and wore enormous Prada dark tortoise shell sunglasses.

The clippety-clop sound of her heels echoed throughout the grey and white marble corridor becoming louder as she reached the glass office and Gemma recognised the shoes immediately. "Jimmy Choos, Chanel suit," said Gemma to herself then changed her mind to Ralph Lauren, no, it's Alexander McQueen.

She had seen the knock-offs in the city's backstreets of Dubai but only the best for 'The Boss', who stopped briefly to peer into the glass-panelled newsroom, momentarily lowering her sunglasses to survey the scene, before pushing them back up onto the bridge of her sharp beak-like nose and then carried on clip-clopping along the corridor until she reached a gold-coloured door.

Gemma watched the woman's long red nails punch in a series of numbers on the keypad signalling the heavy door to swing open allowing her to step inside. Gemma had never been inside her office and, from what she had heard through office gossip, there would be only two reasons - hiring or firing - but it would be interesting just to see what it looked like and meet her news editor-in-chief Yvonne.

It would be good to find out how the 'Black Widow'- the reporters' nickname for her- had got the job especially in a state with strict rules regarding western women. But, then again, maybe too much information would be dangerous as it was rumoured she had Russian mafia connections!

Her immediate line-manager was the news editor Wullie - a tough no-nonsense Scot who was less than complimentary about women; so life for Gemma, as one of a few female reporters, was challenging and demanding.

Her mobile phone rang to a tune of The Proclaimers, reminding her of Scotland and back home in the Ochil Hills in Stirling where she would spend hours hiking, thinking and dreaming of being a successful journalist like her mother, Yasmin, who had worked as a foreign correspondent with The Washington Post. Yasmin had put on hold her glamorous career to settle down and raise Gemma with her archaeologist husband James MacDonald in Kilmartin, on the west coast of Scotland.

Gemma had her father's white blonde hair and green eyes while her mother was Latino, a fiery personality with glossy dark hair and penetrating brown eyes. She remembered her father saying to her as a young child – 'you are descended from the Danes Gemma, never forget that.'

"Would someone answer that phone?" a broad Scots voice boomed from across the newsroom and Gemma instantly recognised it as Wullie's, who resented mobile phones and new technology – "Give me the old type-writers and hot presses any day", was his familiar cry.

"Newsroom, hello... Gemma MacDonald," she said. "So, what's up, sweetheart?" the female voice asked and Gemma smiled. Only Sharon called her pals that.

"Nothing much, slow news day," she replied.

"Well, that's about to change," said the private detective, who was running a highly successful and lucrative business and had an exciting new project to discuss with Gemma.

A year previously, the painful memories of her lost parents had weighed heavily on her mind daily. Despite her grandmother's tender care, Gemma could not escape the hurtful memory. Gemma, who had been working as a freelance journalist for a variety of media outlets in Scotland. She felt something was missing in her life, as indeed it was. Her saving grace was the love of her black horse, Midnight. She needed a fresh start and Sharon had come up with the answer and a place to stay at her glitzy apartment, in the glamorous down-town Dubai.

Midnight, a handsome, proud stallion with a heart of gold, was fast and fearless, theirs was a true bond. Tears welled up in Gemma's emerald-green eyes as she recalled driving to the livery-yard back home in Stirling after finishing work one Friday afternoon.

As she drove her silver-coloured jeep past his field she looked for Midnight, who always recognised the sound of her vehicle, and would come cantering over to the gate waiting to greet her and have his apple titbit. *That's odd,* thought Gemma, *I don't see him. Maybe he's in his stable - but I put him out in the field this morning before I left for work at the office?*

Gemma parked the vehicle, jumped out and opened the boot before taking out a pair of green Wellington boots. Slipping off her black high heeled shoes, she slipped her feet into the cold boots, sending a shiver up her spine.

She walked through the stable area towards the field but could not see Midnight. A quick glance confirmed he was not in his stable. Continuing towards the field as she got closer to the gatepost she spotted a white tape, which divided a large field lay snapped in two on the ground.

As her pace quickened, there, a few yards in front, was her beloved black stallion lying dead on the ground.

She opened her mouth to scream but there was no sound. Her heart began racing so fast she felt like it was going to burst wide open from her chest. Finally, she let out a high-pitched bloodcurdling scream so loud it startled a flock of starlings nestling in the trees nearby causing them to swoop up into the foreboding dark grey sky.

Gemma slumped to the ground, crouched in a foetal position holding her head in her hands rocking back and forth sobbing uncontrollably. "Gemma, Gemma!" She heard a male voice say her name and then felt a strong hand grip the shoulder of her dark brown wax jacket.

After a few seconds she looked up and recognised the face. It was her local vet, Jim, who had been at the livery yard, attending to another horse. He didn't have to tell her the news. Gemma knew by Midnight's facial expression he was dead. "It was a heart attack, Gemma. He didn't suffer. There was nothing anyone could do," he said softly.

Gemma sat there rocking back and forth still refusing to accept what she had just witnessed. Her beloved Midnight was more than just a horse; he was her friend, her soul mate. He had pulled her through after her parents' disappearance. Time stood still when she was at the stables - a place she could forget death and all her troubles. She was numb; her mind a blank. What now?

It had taken Gemma weeks to recover from the loss. She would awaken in the middle of the night convinced Midnight was still alive, galloping together at full speed over the hills, the cool wind caressing her face as they both moved in unison; The thrill of adrenalin flowing through them and joining as one athlete as they raced up and down the undulating terrain, Midnight jumping any ditches or streams they encountered as nimbly as a gazelle.

The feeling of freedom and being at one was incredible and Gemma never wanted it to end. But it always did and now she had decided to have a fresh start in Dubai, thanks to Sharon. 'New horizons,' she had advised.

Gemma had no idea what lay ahead for her in this city full of contrasts and cultures, smells and sights, great opulence and at the same time immense poverty. But she quickly fell in love with the Arabic culture and she loved wandering about the narrow backstreets inhaling the pungent smells wafting from the exotic spices and food in the enveloping heat of the night.

"I've got you in at the stables," Gemma heard a voice she recognized as Sharon's, jolting her back to the present moment.

Gemma had been trying to get an interview with the ruling royal family to write a feature on their remarkable world-class winning record with racehorses but she had drawn a blank and Wullie was beginning to exert pressure on her. The press office at the palace had been extremely unhelpful so Gemma had turned to Sharon to see what she could do.

The pair had met when Gemma interviewed her friend for an article in her newspaper back home as the country's only female private detective agency run by women for women and the feature had made national headlines with a TV special lined up, though it didn't materialise as Sharon had decided to move to Dubai and run her private detective agency there.

A former police chief inspector, Sharon didn't pull any punches. She had developed an iron skin to protect herself in the male-dominated police world and Gemma had too, in the tough profession of journalism where egos ruled. The pair had struck up a common bond and they instantly became the best of friends. It was fair to say they had a connection.

Wullie had challenged Gemma to get the royal racing assignment when she had pitched it, never for one second dreaming she would be able to get the scoop. He had put his other reporters on the job and none of them could pull it off, so he thought it would be a bit of fun watching the 'Wee Mac', as he called her, try and fail.

"I've spoken to my contact with the royal family and he's pulled a few strings to get you in. Anyway, he owes me one and I sold it to him on the good bit of publicity angle and he bought it," said Sharon. "It's who you know don't you know," she exclaimed.

It was the height of summer and hot as hell at fifty degrees and Gemma had never experienced heat like it. She remembered stepping out of the plane at Dubai International Airport at midday and feeling like she was walking into a furnace. She would never forget the hot, dry, heavy desert air filling her nostrils and lungs. She was grateful for the cooling air conditioning of the white taxi which whisked her through the city streets lined with skyscraper-mirrored buildings to Sharon's apartment.

"Fantastic, where and when?" replied Gemma already thinking of a heading for the feature - 'Secrets to a Successful Royal Racing Dynasty'. *Hope I can uncover some,* she thought to herself.

"Tomorrow, at the royal stables, outside Jaball City, Qamar, 8am," said Sharon.

"Thanks. Are we still on for tomorrow night's curry?" asked Gemma.

"I wouldn't miss it. See you there," said Sharon, desperately trying to stick to her diet but decided the best way to deal with temptation was to give in to it! She could smell the mouth-watering aroma of saffron and cumin as she walked through the Spice Souk talking to Gemma on her mobile phone, her stomach rumbling and realising she had only had a diet banana milk shake for breakfast.

Feeling pleased, Gemma walked across the spacious open-plan newsroom towards Wullie's office. The door was open (that meant the bar was shut) and she knocked politely and insistently. Wullie sat behind his large, white desk- his red face blazed like an electric fire. He must have been dipping into the 'electric soup' as they say in Scotland. Secretly, he took a slug of malt whisky, from a black hipflask with a silver screw top which he hid in the bottom drawer of his desk.

"Ah Wee Mac, have you got anywhere with the royals and their nags?" he grinned at Gemma through yellow teeth that had seen better days. Years of chain smoking and hard drinking had taken their toll on his health but he refused to change his habits now, apart from the smoking, as it was banned in the building.

He was forced to go out onto the rooftop for a fly puff, refusing to look down as he was scared stiff of heights - a throwback to his childhood when he was stranded on the roof of a red brick tower block of flats at his home in Glasgow. He had never forgotten the feelings of fear and helplessness and to this day heights scared the living daylights out of him but he did it anyway as his addiction always won.

"Actually yes," replied Gemma, smoothing down her white blonde hair. She was medium height and athletic with a pretty heart-shaped face but her incredibly sparkling emerald green eyes were her best feature.

"You have?" said a startled Wullie.

"Yes, I have to meet King Aariz tomorrow at the royal stables," Gemma replied.

"Are you sure?" he asked, feeling frustrated that he was not going to have the satisfaction of seeing her struggle. Gathering his thoughts and trying to hide his disappointment he said: "About time. This is what we'll do." He knew that the feature would get circulation up and he was coming under increasing pressure from madam (that's what he called Yvonne, the editor-in-chief) at the paper's daily conference.

"Right, lassie, I want 1500 words on Ali and his nags and take boy wonder with you and get some great pics," he growled reaching down to the handle of the bottom drawer again.

Gemma felt her cheeks getting redder with sheer anger, and she wanted to shout a variety of colourful language at him, like the male reporters back home, but as the saying goes revenge is a dish best served cold.

"I want a picture spread. It's going to be 'A Royal Racing Dynasty'. What a heading," he complemented himself, before sifting through the news schedule for the day.

She was about to say that the King was called Aariz, not Ali but thought, what's the point? As she turned to go she heard him say: "If this works out I'll let you make my coffee from now on!"

When Gemma reached the door and with her hand on the handle she turned and replied: "Do you want a coffee now?"...

He looked startled. "Aye, OK!"

Gemma smiled: "Sorry, too busy," she replied sharply before closing the door as he gasped out loud. She looked over at Kevin, a tall, lanky Geordie with a mop of curly dark hair, who was perched on the end of his light brown desk examining his shiny black digital camera and gently rubbing the lens with a soft, grey-coloured cloth.

He was shy, but great with the camera and Gemma had liked him immediately as he had shown her around when she first arrived at the office.

"He's not worth bothering about," Kevin turned to Gemma, who could feel the warmth on her cheeks. "Look he's half cut and I hear he's on his way out if he makes any more cock-ups."

"I heard what he said. I'll meet you in the office tomorrow at 6.45am and we can take the company jeep," he said.

"Okay," Gemma sighed, still smarting at the way Wullie had spoken to her. Count to ten ... she had reminded herself.

The Next Day

"Come on, Gemma we'd better get started. There's not much time and I want to catch this soft light. We need to get over to the stables ASAP," said Kevin jumping up off his desk and heading towards the smoky brown tinted-glass door towards the elevator.

"Okay, I'm coming. Give me a minute," she said, smoothing down her beige linen trousers and matching jacket before pulling down the brim of her matching wide-brimmed hat and putting the strap of her brown leather handbag over her shoulder. She then checked to make sure her notebook, recorder and mobile phone were there.

After a couple of hours they arrived at the Royal Stables in Jaball; just as the horses were being prepared for the early-morning gallops.

As Gemma stepped outside the jeep the sweet smell of hay brought back memories of Midnight and galloping over the Ochil Hills. The feeling of total exhilaration and speed and being at one with such an incredible powerful beast was amazing and it simply took her breath away.

She wandered into a stable block of what must have housed one hundred horses at least. The cool air conditioning was welcome and caressed her face and body. It felt fantastic and she breathed it in, sighing deeply.

"The wind in heaven is that which blows between a horse's ears," said a deep male voice with a slight Arabic accent.

"Is that so?" said Gemma slightly startled, peering over a stable door at a figure mucking out next to an impressive looking powerfully-built black Arabian stallion which was casually munching hay from an orange - coloured net.

"It's an old Arabic proverb," said the young man, with his back to her, picking up dung with a pitchfork and tossing it into a green-coloured wheelbarrow.

"I'm Gemma MacDonald from the Emirates Chronicle."

A stable-hand peered at Gemma through the black iron bars at the top of the stable door, and admired her blonde hair and intelligent face. He stroked Dancer's gleaming neck and then looked back at Gemma.

"I'm doing a feature on Sheik Aariz and his race-horses and I was told to come here this morning," said Gemma. The man walked out of the stable, bolted the door behind him, securing a lead rope to the fastening.

Walking a few paces along the stable corridor, Gemma reached inside her bag to double check her mobile was there. She then felt a warm sensation on her neck. Turning around she saw a lovely-looking light grey horse with a mischievous look in its pale blue eye.

"You like horses?" The young man asked.

"Yes, very much," replied Gemma."She's a superb filly," said Gemma, stroking the horse between her eyes, a sweet spot where a mare calms her foal. "What's her name?" asked Gemma.

"Blossom, Apple Blossom, pure as the driven snow," replied Abdul. Gemma was looking at the mare's other eye which was dark blue and thought it was incredibly unusual.

"Her mother was a champion racehorse as was her sire Dancer," said the young man proudly. "She is to race in the Jaball Gold Cup," he said. Gemma knew it was THE event of the year in the social calendar and attracted racehorses from all over the world to compete for the coveted trophy and prestige of winning the great race.

"Do you work here?" she asked looking around.

"You could say that. I'm sorry but I have been asked if you can return tomorrow as the King has been detained on some urgent business." There was a pause and he added: "We did call your office?"

Wullie! Just the sort of thing he would do, thought Gemma. She frowned, knowing Wullie wanted the story as soon as possible but thought again, *let him wait.*

"Okay, do you mind if we take a few pictures while we are here?" she asked.

"I'm sure it will be okay with my boss," he replied. "See you at five am," said the man.

Five am, thought Gemma, *and I've got dinner with Sharon and I'll have to 'update' Wullie though I suspect he'll be expecting it.*

"See you tomorrow," he said turning to walk away pushing the wheelbarrow full of muck along the long corridor.

"Okay, what's your name?" Gemma shouted after him but there was only the sound of horses whinnying and her voice echo fading away.

It had been a long day and Gemma was enjoying dinner with Sharon at the exclusive Indian restaurant - Shamin's - which was the 'talk of the steamie' and they both laughed at the Scots term for the old-fashioned washhouse; where women cleaned the families' clothes communally and gossiped to pass the monotonous task and she imagined this was a parallel with river washing in other countries.

Gemma began scraping the last morsel of Garlic Chilli Chicken off her plate. She loved it but knew tomorrow would be another story - garlic breath and interviewing were not a good combination but for now she was enjoying herself and pondering over Sharon's latest idea.

She had already started to think about a chaperone service for women run by women, escorting visitors coming to Dubai who would want a female guide to show them the sights, restaurants, souks and shops. There were no better bargains in the world than right here and Sharon knew the best places to go.

"Okay, so how are we going to do this?" asked Gemma leaning back in her seat, feeling happy, relaxing and stretching her tanned legs out in front of her.

"I'm thinking, you organize all the media, promo side of things and I'll get the staff," said Sharon dipping a piece of Naan bread into the reddish orange-coloured sauce.

"No problem," said Gemma. "I've already got a few ideas and if you take care of the practical side of the business then we're quids in."

"Agreed," said Gemma. "Put it there," said Sharon shaking Gemma's hand.

"Wullie is a right pain in the ass. He gave me such a hard time over the 'Ali' interview but I managed to calm down his faux outrage. I told him of the rescheduled date, promising I would get a more in-depth feature article tomorrow. Just hope I do or my jacket is on a 'shooglie-peg' as they say," continued Gemma.

Sharon laughed and Gemma joined in. She is such a good friend, thought Gemma, I am lucky.

"Come on let's go. I've got a really early start tomorrow at the race track," said Gemma standing up before pushing away the ornately carved golden chair.

In the Mountains of South Qamar

The old man was camped near the mouth of the cave high in the mountains. As the sun threatened to rise, as it had so many times before, the stars faded into infinity.

The long shadows grew and shortened and for a while it looked as if the mountain range was sprinkled with caves. The old man and many others before him had witnessed the same spectacle many times over until their time ended and another had taken their place. It had always been that way. Life has a way of compensating for such dedication.

None of this mattered. There was only one cave and one purpose. It seemed like he had lived in these mountains forever as did all who came before him – way back further than he could remember in fact and legend. Yet none of this concerned him. Time had made him part of the landscape and he, too, felt part of it.

In the nearest village - some twenty miles away in the foothills - where he and his family had originated, the people certainly thought of him and his family that way.

The people of the village had admired the eons of dedication and sometimes feared its intention. To be feared and cursed was their fate. They kept their distance.

As the sun ascended over the mountaintops it kissed his face as he sat facing east. There was no heat in the sun at this time but his faith warmed him. Few travelled these mountains, mostly goat-herders or caravans heading along the spice trail of old seeking the coast.

He greeted the few to encounter him with a wave of acknowledgment of indifference. Infrequently, he would share tea with those who passed by and they would tell him of the changes they had seen and what they knew of the world. He accepted all with a kind smile and nodding politely. It is hard to make conversation when you do not do so frequently. Perhaps, it was because he had so little in common with the outside world as they knew it.

There were bandits in these mountains and wild creatures too. He did not fear them as he was no threat to them and had nothing of value. They accepted he simply was. The only thing they had in common was they belonged to the land.

Ever since his early ancestors had discovered the crystal they knew it had a journey to make and would, eventually, return to the cave. Until now they had watched and waited.

'What comes from the earth, must surely return there' they told each other. He was the last of his family as he had no children. As he waited, he wondered what that meant.

Chapter Two

Qamar state - Flying Palace

It was the day of the interview. Gemma felt the butterflies fluttering about in her stomach and tried to keep them under control. It was her big break - her article on King Aariz and his world-renowned racing dynasty. No western journalist had ever had access or interviewed him before about his beloved racehorses.

Gemma wanted to uncover why and how he bred such incredible animals which won time and time again in the top races throughout the world. What was the winning formula? Was there a secret to his success? If there was she had to find it and get the news angle for this feature. She was hungry and determined to prove Wullie wrong about her.

Gemma and Kevin arrived at the racecourse just after five am. They were both feeling a bit tired but looking forward to their assignment. While they were waiting for the King to arrive, Gemma perked up after watching a group of racehorses being put through their paces at the early morning gallops. This was the best time of day; the temperature comfortable outside before it rose to an unbearable heat, like walking into a furnace, Sharon once said, and she was right.

Just then Kevin motioned to Gemma pointing over to his right. "Look over there," he said. Gemma could just make out the three black vehicles approaching the stable gates followed by a cloud of golden sand whirling through the air.

Two men dressed in black suits and wearing sunglasses emerged from the first and last vehicles and took up positions. Then Gemma watched as the front passenger of the middle vehicle got out and opened the rear door. A man dressed in white robes emerged smiling and walked over towards Gemma and Kevin accompanied by a younger man.

"Miss MacDonald from the Chronicle, I presume," the King asked.

"Yes," replied Gemma, "It's a pleasure to meet you, Your Majesty," she added, shaking his outstretched hand.

"Thank you for taking time out of your busy schedule for this interview," said Gemma.

"I'm sorry for having to cancel yesterday but matters of state, you understand."

"Of course," replied Gemma.

The King replied: "I have time for a few pictures here and perhaps you can accompany me to the international airport in Dubai before I depart?"

"Yes, that would be great," replied Gemma.

"I understand you met my son, Abdul, yesterday," asked the King.

Son? Gemma thought. "We weren't formally introduced," said Gemma looking over at a now-smiling Abdul.

"This is my photographer, Kevin," said Gemma.

"Pleased to meet you, Your Majesty," he said shaking the King's hand. "If it's okay with you King Aariz I think a picture of yourself with two of your prize race horses would make a great shot for the article. Can I suggest we shoot at the stable entrance where the ornate gates with the royal seal and the King Aariz nameplate are? I think that would be a fantastic backdrop," said Kevin excitedly.

"Abdul, can you arrange for the horses to be brought over to the gate?" asked the King.

"Of course, my father," replied Abdul striding towards the stables.

Meanwhile, the King and Gemma walked towards the stable gates. "I have to say that when I visited your stables yesterday I was impressed with the layout and tiling and even the air conditioning. That's not something I have ever seen before at a yard," said Gemma.

"You have horses Ms MacDonald?" asked King Aariz.

"I did have but he passed away," replied Gemma.

"I know how painful that can be. Our horses are like family. My ancestors would keep their Arabian mares and foals in their Bedouin tents which is why there is such a close bond between us.

"Did you know the Arabian is the oldest domesticated horse on the planet? It is fast, strong and fearless in battle. Through the centuries it has had to adapt and survive in the desert, like ourselves," he said.

Gemma thought about the correlation. It made sense. We have to work together in order to survive.

When they arrived at the main entrance the horses were there with their handlers. The King placed himself between the two horses holding the lead reins and the handlers stepped back out of the picture. Kevin went to work and after a short time they had finished.

In the distance they could hear the buzzing of a helicopter as it made its way closer. One of the security guards touched his ear piece. "Your Majesty, touch down within a minute," he said.

"If it's okay with you, Your Majesty, Kevin would like to stay here and take more pictures.

"Yes, replied the King. One off my staff will escort him."

The King and his bodyguards, Gemma and Abdul then left in the vehicles and headed for the helipad to catch the helicopter bound for Dubai International Airport.

After a forty-minute flight they set down at the airport near a huge white aircraft with the Dubai royal crest emblazoned on it.

The party disembarked from the helicopter and Gemma followed the King, Abdul and the escort over to the large aircraft where they were greeted by the Captain and his crew. After a brief exchange the King and his party boarded the aircraft.

As Gemma stepped inside the massive aeroplane she noticed several horses in stalls nearby. She was in awe by the sheer size of the interior and the opulence inside observing the orange and cream sofas with beige cushions. As Gemma walked on the plush, deep-pile beige carpet she noticed pictures of racehorses on the walls and a huge photograph of the ocean with white horses dancing on the surface.

Moving into another area with more settees she marvelled at the massive dining room and bar with eight huge flat-screen televisions.

Abdul laughed at Gemma's wide-eyed expression. "Wait till you see the wellness area," he said leading her into a private lounge area with the royal crest embroidered on the soft comfortable cream seats.

"Please take a seat," said Abdul. "My father will be here shortly. I have ordered some refreshments." They entered the dining room and sat down at the long table which could easily seat sixteen people. Gemma was still too stunned to say thanks. The place was incredible - a flying palace - *wait till I tell Sharon about this and what a story!* she thought.

King Aariz entered the room accompanied by a man in long flowing white robes. "I hope Abdul has seen that you are comfortable," said the King. "Please be seated," he motioned to them at the table.

"This is Aquil, my advisor," said King Aariz. Aquil barely acknowledged Gemma's presence as he was annoyed the King had given his permission for an interview with the newspaper. He didn't want him to be given good publicity but Abdul had persuaded his father otherwise and there was nothing he could do about it.

The King sat at the top of the clear glass rectangular table. Gemma looked at Aquil noticing he was of average build, with dark hair, piercing narrow brown eyes with a deep scar running down the left side of his cheek and he commanded a foreboding presence. He sat himself next to the King.

After a sumptuous lunch, the staff began clearing away and they continued the interview and Gemma found the King's story to be fascinating.

She learned about his Bedouin heritage, trading with the Norsemen, his passion for his horses, racing and subjects, and plans for a greener environment for Qamar. He came across as a man who cared about his land and his people. "Tell me about your people and where your love of horses began, Sire?"

"Horses have been a vital part of my family through the generations of Bedouins. We have matured and succeeded together. We came from the desert, from humble beginnings and together with our relationship with the Arabians we have grown and evolved."

Just then the King's mobile phone went off and he answered and spoke a few words in Arabic. "Excuse me, I must take this call. Please excuse me," he said before walking out of the dining room followed by a body-guard.

"Tell me about you, Gemma," said Abdul, reaching over to the bowl of brown dates on the coffee table before popping one into his mouth.

"Well, I was born in Scotland and when your father mentioned the Norsemen, specifically Vikings, I remembered my grandmother telling me stories about the Norsemen in Scotland and when they raided the west coast centuries ago. She told me I was descended from the Danes and that I was born with a hallihoo," said Gemma.

"What is that?" asked Abdul.

"It's a piece of skin around a baby's head and is said to be lucky, sometimes called a 'holy hood'," replied Gemma. "My grandmother used to keep it in the family bible."

Aquil stopped and stared straight ahead thinking to himself how ludicrous the story was. And yet, he seemed to recognize a certain resonance about this comment, he noted for later. Abdul laughed at the thought and Gemma smiled. "I know it sounds bit ridiculous."

"Yes, we have some old customs too, don't we Aquil?" said Abdul looking over at his father's adviser, who remained disinterested. Gemma looked over at a bored-looking Aquil who was now browsing through his black tablet.

After a few moments, Abdul said: "Aquil."

"Yes, your Highness, we certainly do," before rising from the couch bed to follow the King and thinking about Abdul's twin brother Khalid and his next meeting with him.

Just then Gemma's phone rang and a familiar name flashed up on the screen. "Excuse me, do you mind?" she asked indicating her mobile phone.

"Not at all," replied Abdul politely. Gemma stood up and wandered along the compartment.

"So what are you up to Cuz?" asked Gemma visualising her cousin Sparks surrounded by a myriad of gadgets in his New York premises.

"Working on my latest invention, busy, busy, busy! It's so cool and I know you will just love it."

"I believe you," replied Gemma thinking of her gangly, pale-faced, red-haired, geeky cousin who was a whiz with technology.

"I want to send some samples of my latest inventions so you can try them out and see what you think. What's your address over there?" he asked and Gemma told him Sharon's address.

"This delivery will have to be handed to you personally and signed for. How are you enjoying the job?" he asked.

"I'm on a King's private jet interviewing him for a feature in the paper. It's fascinating stuff," said Gemma.

"I can't wait to read it. Send me a copy," teased Sparks. "I will brief you on your new toys and I've sent the operating instructions to your telephone. When will be convenient for you?"

Gemma replied: "Later this evening about 10pm Dubai time, I should think."

"That's fine. I'll see you then! Gotta go, I've another idea to write down before I forget," he said.

"Okay, bye for now, Sparkie," said Gemma, ending the call and wondering what he was going to be sending her, and his cryptic use of 'See you then.'

As Gemma returned to join Abdul at the table, a waiter, dressed in a pristine white uniform trimmed with gold, approached and placed a glass filled with blue liquid decorated with an orange flower on the rim. Abdul noticed small beads of sweat forming on the man's face, which was odd as the air conditioning on the jet made the air quite cool. Just then Abdul's nostrils filled with a familiar smell.

Where had he smelled that before? In England, at training camp! His father had sent Abdul and Khalid to an elite military academy where they were also trained in self-defence and weapons handling.

It was the smell of gun oil Abdul used to clean his German Sig Sauer handgun he recognised. He watched as the waiter slid his hand underneath the white napkin. *That's odd,* he thought, before he lunged at the man, throwing him onto a glass coffee table.

Gemma moved over to where the two figures were grappling and struggling. She had no idea what had happened but knew she had to intercede. It was then she saw the pistol. Galvanised into action, Gemma decided to take action. Stepping over to the handgun she smartly kicked it towards Abdul and his attacker.

Crash, bang, thump! She sees Abdul being pushed down further, two hands around his neck began squeezing tighter, the veins sticking up. Abdul, who saw the pistol, picked it up, hit the man on the head with it knocking him unconscious.

"Are you okay, Gemma?" asked Abdul getting up off the floor and walking over towards Gemma who was sitting on the carpet, legs outstretched breathing deeply. Ripping a gold chord from a pair of curtains he secured the man's hands behind his back.

"I'm fine. I'm just recovering from the shock. I've never been involved in anything like this before," she said.

"If you hadn't kicked that gun over to me it may have been a different story," said Abdul with a wry smile. "Wait, didn't you say you were from Scotland?"

"Isn't it dangerous to fire a gun in an aircraft? I thought the bullets would depressurise the cabin," asked Gemma.

"That's only when we are in the air," replied Abdul. "If they are specialised rounds of low power or squash-head nature, like the kind our bodyguards carry when we are flying, they wouldn't affect the aircraft's pressure but that was not an issue here," he continued.

"Did I just witness an assassination attempt or is this another of your pranks? Who is he? What is going on? " asked Gemma, sighing deeply.

"I would appreciate it if you didn't mention his incident to anyone," said Abdul sitting down on the leather couch.

But it's a great story! Gemma thought to herself, *how can I not report it?* Abdul could see by the expression on Gemma's face that she was thinking about the story.

"Let me explain. This isn't the first time this has happened. My father has many enemies and we wouldn't want to put him a position of weakness.

"Why did you tackle him?" asked Gemma.

"When he entered the lounge and walked over to place a drink at my table I noticed beads of sweat. It is pleasantly cool and I smelled something odd. Sweet and yet, out-of-place ... *something from the past* I wondered? It's special oil used for cleaning and maintaining certain weapons."

Abdul pressed the emergency button and Aquil and two bodyguards appeared. Abdul handed the gun to Aquil and said: "This man just tried to kill us. I need to know how this was allowed to happen on a private aircraft with our security."

The two bodyguards picked up the unconscious assailant and removed him from the aircraft followed by Aquil. Just then the King appeared. "Are you alright, my son, I've just heard what's happened? The King asked."

"I'm fine, but thanks to Gemma it was a close shave," he replied. "In view of what's happened are you sure you should go on this trip?" asked Abdul.

"It's a visit long in the planning and it's of great importance to the future of Qamar and our people, my son," he replied. Thank you Ms MacDonald for what you did. My sincere apologies to you, for cutting our interview short and my everlasting thanks and gratitude for what you have done for my son. When I return we can continue our dialogue. It has been most interesting and enjoyable."

"Yes, of course, thank you, I mean, *Shukran jazilan.*"

Abdul and Gemma both wished the King a pleasant and safe journey and disembarked from the aircraft. "Do you think your father will be alright," asked Gemma.

"I don't know. I can't be sure. He has his security but after what happened …"

As they headed towards one of the vehicles Abdul asked Gemma: "Where to now?"

"I'm due back at the paper. Can you drop me off please?"

"Yes, of course," replied Abdul the recent events still weighing on his mind.

During the journey Gemma asked Abdul about the Bedouins and their relationship with horses and racing. "Earlier your father mentioned the pure bloodline. Why is that?" Gemma asked.

Abdul began to tell the story of the legendary Bedouin horse race which began centuries ago in his Kingdom.

500 years ago – Middle East

Five of the goats were missing. Malik counted them all again. Fifteen and there should be twenty. His father would be mad if he lost even one. He couldn't go home to the village without them.

Malik stopped at the rocky outcrop, sat down and could just make out a faint jingling sound. He got up and walked over in the direction of the noise, bent down at one of the sandy rocks and he could see an opening just big enough for him to squeeze his slight body through. He peered inside and spotted what looked like a goat's tail and proceeded to go through the gap. *"I must get the goats back and quickly before the rest of the herd wander too far,"* he thought before scrambling through to the other side.

He saw the goats nearby drinking from a small pool of water. "There you are. Come, hurry up. We must get back before it gets dark," he spoke to the goats, which all looked up at him in unison, before he noticed something flickering in the pool. It looked like silver wings and it was the most beautiful thing he had ever seen, shimmering and glistening in the clear water.

Malik reached in with his hand and quickly drew it out. When he opened his clasped hand his look of disappointment was clear. Just then the goats ran out through the opening and Malik ran after them thrusting the object into his trouser pocket.

The sound of a tinkling bell, worn by the lead goat, broke the silence in the cool night air as Malik made his way back to the village where he was born. The prestigious and renowned Bedouin horse race over relentless terrain - when tribes from all over the area travelled to compete - was being held in the not too distant future and Malik was desperate to compete and win the prize of the best of the losers' herds.

How Malik longed to help his father and family have a better life. The Bedouins were a simple people who had true values in life and respect for each other and the land was paramount to them.

He reached into his pocket and pulled out his hand unfurling it and looked at the smooth white pebble. It looked so ordinary and yet he could sense somehow that it was special.

"You know Malik," said his father turning to his son after returning with the goatherd. "I want only the best for you, you know that my son?"

As they shared their evening meal his father spoke: "If we had the mare then we would have the race. You know there is no price put on the head of a prized war mare and we need that, you understand Malik, don't you?"

"I know, my father, I must go. I will leave tomorrow before sunrise," replied Malik walking over to some camels to prepare them for their journey.

Next morning his father bade him farewell. "*Inchallah* (God willing}," replied his father, tears welling up in his sad brown eyes as he watched his young son leave with the goods to trade for the mare. He was a good boy and knew this day would come when he would leave and hopefully return with the mare to take part in the race.

Malik had been travelling for several days and at 50 degrees during the day it was too hot to travel so it was common practice for travellers then rested and went on the move at night, being guided by the stars. Malik could remember his father's voice saying: *'Look for the Ursa Major (The Great Bear) and it will lead you to the Polaris' (northern star). "The map is inside your head, Malik. Always remember this,"* he could hear his father's words echoing in his thoughts.

Looking at the pink dewy haze above the horizon he surveyed the sand dunes to help him on his journey. He was heading for the town and he had goods with him to trade for a mare.

Ahead he could see a large brown dust cloud in the distance and he knew it was trouble. There was nowhere to run and no escape. He commanded his camel to kneel down. Malik then dismounted, urging the camel to lie down beside the other camel carrying the goods, extra water and food supplies while Malik lay against its belly covering his face and keeping his lips shut tightly while waiting for the inevitable to happen.

He watched as the dust devil came nearer, the howling wind whipping up the sand in a frenzied motion, swirling upwards into a tight cylindrical shape carrying it across the vast plain and blotting out the sun.

Reaching into his pocket Malik clutched the smooth white pebble and prayed for a miracle. The wind ceased and all was quiet. Slowly, Malik unfurled the scarf around his face. He was buried under a mountain of golden sand and began furiously digging for air until he saw daylight. Fortunately, his camel had survived but the other, with the supplies, was lost without trace and the drifting sand was too deep to explore any further.

He still had the goatskin water container which was full but he knew he would need to get more and soon. Just as he was about to get on the camel Malik spotted a red and white checked object nearby. As he got closer he recognised the *Keffiyeh* and then saw a hand sticking out of the sand. He bent down and began digging, frantically shovelling off mounds of sand from the body below. Malik found the man's pulse. It was still beating, albeit faintly, and he needed to get help and soon.

Malik took out the water container and poured the water over the man's face. His brown eyes opened briefly and Malik put the container to his pale white cracked lips and the man took a few gulps.

Not too much, thought Malik, before carrying him over to his camel which was kneeling down. Summoning up all his strength Malik lifted the limp body onto his camel, mounted and summoned it to stand up. After what seemed like hours travelling across the vast desert, Malik saw the familiar outline on the horizon and breathed a sigh of relief hoping that he wasn't too late.

Their arrival caused a commotion at the Bedouin campsite. The man was taken into one of the tents and the Bedouins ushered Malik into a smaller one giving him food and water, as was the custom, even if you were an enemy.

Malik was tired and weary and fell fast asleep. Much later, he was woken by a Bedouin, carrying tea. "You have been asleep for many hours," said the woman.

"How is the man? Is he still alive?" asked Malik.

"Yes, but he is still weak," she replied offering him a bowl of water and cloth for washing. Malik was feeling stiff and sore from the journey. "Come outside when you are ready," said the woman before leaving the tent.

Several minutes later Malik stepped outside the tent and wandered over to a man with a bright chestnut horse which had no saddle or bridle and only a rope halter with a white rope attached to it.

The man then reversed the horse backwards and forwards and sideways before coming to a stop and stroking the horse on its sweet spot between its eyes.

The man turned to Malik: "Come closer," he said handing the rope to Malik. The horse jumped back but Malik stood his ground and copied what the man did releasing and applying pressure until the horse snorted several times.

"Very good, you see he is releasing his pent-up tension." said the man. "This is Ramsez, one our prized stallions. He has covered many mares but only the purest lines. Do you know that the best war horses are Arabian mares?" he asked leading the horse over for a drink of water from the open pot at the well.

"No, why is that?" asked Malik.

"Because they show great courage in battle and bravely take the spear thrust without giving ground. They also don't wicker to our enemies' horses during raids which would act as a warning. A war mare has no price and there is no greater gift for a Bedouin than an Arabian mare.

My name is Buraq," said the man.

"Malik," Malik replied.

"*Marhaban,*" (welcome) Buraq replied. "Let's have some tea." Malik followed Buraq and Ramsez over to another one of the tents and watched as Buraq put

Ramsez in one part of the tent before ushering Malik to sit down.

"So, tell me who you are and how you came to be in my gratitude," said Buraq pouring golden brown liquid from an ornate silver pewter teapot into two small matching cups.

"There's not much to tell. I come from a small village in the north and tend to my father's goats but one day I will win the desert race for my family," he said.

"That is a very fine ambition," said Buraq.

"I was going to trade to buy a horse to ride in the race but I lost everything in the sandstorm," said Malik.

"I see. And can you ride?" asked Buraq.

"Well no, but I'm a quick learner and I'm strong," replied Malik.

"You know it is a dangerous race. Many who take part will die. You need much strength and courage and, of course, Allah's blessing," Buraq told him standing up and pondering a while. "Perhaps you would like to stay here for a while as our guest? We have plenty of food and shelter and you can work with the horses."

Malik's face lit up and smiled. "Yes, I would like that."

Over the next few weeks Buraq showed Malik his horse handling skills and Malik was a fast and keen learner. Even when he fell off dozens of times, Malik brushed himself down and got right back up on the horse again and carried on.

One morning Malik was tacking up his favourite mare Destiny. She had thrown him more than any of the other horses but there was something about her that he liked and found it difficult to be cross with, even when his body was covered in bruises when he hit the ground.

He turned around and saw Buraq approaching. "It's time for you to leave, Malik. I cannot teach you anymore. You must experience it for yourself," he said.

Malik felt sad as he had enjoyed his experience at the camp but at the same time missed his family and village.

Taking the reins in one hand Buraq placed them in Malik's left hand. "She is yours - a gift for saving my son. This mare is *Asil* (of pure blood) and she must not be bred with a stallion of impure blood. Promise me you will keep the bloodline pure?"

"Of course, I promise, Buraq. I can't thank you enough for all you have done for me. She is a fine mare," replied Buraq beaming with happiness.

"Go in peace, said Buraq. She has caused you the most trouble, but the most difficult ones to control are the most worthy," Buraq added. He watched the young boy ride off into the desert leaving behind a cloud of dust. He watched for a long time until the tiny figures disappeared across the horizon and prayed to Allah - they would need all the luck they could get.

Malik returned safely to his village and, after telling his father what had happened, began preparing in earnest for the race of the year.

He trained Destiny for weeks before the big event, riding up and down the mountains to strengthen her back and rump muscles, and short sprint work, though not too much as he didn't want her to pull a ligament or, far worse, a tendon.

After one training session as Malik was cooling Destiny down with water, his father approached: "Not long now, Malik. Is she ready?" he asked.

"As ready as she will ever be," Malik replied pouring more water over her neck and flanks, removing the excess with a cloth, and then giving her a small amount of water to drink. He would feed her later once she had recovered from the workout.

The race was in a few days' time so he would give Destiny a day off tomorrow so that she was fit and ready for the event. It was not a particularly long route but the terrain, mountainous in parts, was tricky and it was going to be a tough challenge.

He led Destiny into his tent and gave her a feed before going into his tent to eat a light supper before retiring. He was feeling drained after the intensive training schedule and after his meal fell fast asleep.

Sometime later he awoke and rose to make sure Destiny had enough water but to his horror discovered she had gone. He ran out of the black tent and searched the campsite but there was no trace of her.

His father approached. "We must find her," Malik urged him. "*Where could she be? Who could've taken her*?" thoughts racing through his mind.

The pair searched for hoof prints leading from the tent and began tracking. There were two sets of hoof prints and one horse was carrying a rider.

Why did I fall asleep, thought Malik? *I should have put a guard on her, but it's too late worrying about that now.* All their hopes lay on the race ... *I must get her back somehow.*

Saddling up a grey horse, Malik picked up the trail praying he would get to the mare before it was too late. Why she was stolen wasn't important right now. Malik rode until dusk and prayed he would find her. It was getting more difficult to follow the trail with the light fading but he spotted that the tracks had stopped at the crescent-shaped dunes.

Malik dismounted and crawled over on his hands and knees and saw two horses and a man. He recognised Destiny straight away and also the other horse and realised it was the chestnut stallion Ramzes from the Bedouin camp.

As darkness fell, the night sky became a sea of sparkling, twinkling stars. Slowly and stealthily Malik crept up beside the man who was lying on the sand. The horses had sensed Malik was approaching and became agitated, pawing the ground and straining at the tethers around their fetlocks.

Malik seized his chance and jumped on top of the thief, the pair struggling and fighting in the deep sand. Just as Malik was about to seize him by the neck he tripped and stumbled onto the ground. Before he could get back up again, Malik caught the glint of steel to his right.

As the robber drew the dagger up above his head, Malik knew there was no chance of escape. He was pinned down and couldn't move. Then he heard the sound of hooves and looked up to see Destiny in full rear up above the thief's head bringing the full force of her weight on top of him.

Malik jumped up and went over to the man, feeling for his pulse, nothing. Dropping the lifeless arm, Malik then headed over to Destiny and threw his arms around the mare's neck. She backed off which was unusual. As he broke away he looked down at his white blood-stained robe and looked in horror at the wound in her chest.

Quickly, he went over and grabbed the water container to wash the wound and pressed a damp cloth firmly over it to stem the flow of blood. It was still seeping and Malik knew he had to stop it and quickly. He reached into his pocket and took out the smooth white pebble and without knowing why placed it over the wound.

Suddenly, there was a flash of white light and the pebble changed into a clear crystal in the shape of a winged horse. Slowly, the blood flow stopped until there was not one drop left. Malik reached to grasp the clear crystal from the wound, which had miraculously vanished leaving no scar. As he opened the palm of his hand he looked down at the smooth white pebble staring in amazement at what had just happened.

Destiny bent down and licked his face, nuzzling into his neck. He would never forget she saved his life and she would not forget he had saved hers. Their bond was sealed in that moment and couldn't be broken.

The day of the race had finally arrived and Malik was trying hard not to feel nervous but the butterflies in the pit of his stomach were telling him otherwise. Bedouin tribes had travelled from far and wide for the race of the year and it was also a time to get together for a social occasion to discuss bloodlines, greyhounds, falconry and poetry with other each other.

It was just before dawn and the race would start soon before the searing sun bore down on the desert landscape, its fierce rays showing no mercy to man or beast at the height of the day.

Just as Malik was tacking up Destiny, who was in perfect health despite her earlier injury, a rider approached him. He was tall with a deep scar which ran from across his left eye to the right corner of his mouth.

Immediately, Malik winced as he had heard tales of the scar-faced warrior who terrorised his enemies and showed them no mercy. His name was Fahd, or 'The Panther', a cruel and evil man who would stop at nothing to get what he wanted.

"So, you think you have a chance racing against us?" Fahd came closer so Malik could see the deep creases at the edges of his cold, piercing steely eyes as black as coal.

"My mare has never lost and neither have I. It may be wise for you to re-consider," he hissed at Malik. Fahd had heard what happened to the thief in the desert and the boy had shown great courage. He could well be a threat but he would not tolerate the possibility of being beaten. The other riders also knew of Fahd's reputation and were praying something would happen to him or the horse during the race.

"Come, it is time for the race," said one of the stewards ushering Malik forward and then stopping in his tracks when he saw it was Fahd.

"Forgive me. I did not know it was you, Fahd," he stammered.

"Ach, never mind. I will crush you both if you don't die in the race," said Fahd turning around and striding over to his black mare.

"It would be foolish to cross him," said the steward. Malik took up the reins, jumped up on Destiny, and trotted over to the starting area thinking about what Fahd had said.

The starter was trying to get the competitors and their mounts to stand in a line but it was proving difficult. One horse had thrown its rider and galloped off, much to the anger of the jockey and owner. Several others kept breaking the line.

Finally, the signal went up and they were off thundering across the desert and heading for the imposing beige mountains in the distance.

By the time the field reached the mountains they had spread out and slowed up slightly over the rocky terrain. The riders wound their way up the steep path, along the mountain top and back down into the flat desert. The arduous terrain had taken its toll on many horses and riders who had either fallen off or pulled up through injury or sheer exhaustion.

Only a handful remained including Malik and Fahd, who was driving his horse mercilessly on and on. Malik had been careful not to push Destiny too much in the mountains but Fahd was riding like a man possessed.

Menna watched as he could see some riders returning towards the camp and desperately tried to see if one of them was Malik but they were still too far away to make out.

Destiny had gained ground and was ahead of the rest of the field taking it all in her stride and loving every minute of it. It wasn't far now, Malik thought to himself as he could make out the tents in the distance and was feeling confident until he felt a stinging searing pain across his back and felt like he had been cut with a knife.

Turning around he saw it was Fahd with a long leather whip. Again he felt a sharp stinging pain, this time across his shoulder.

In an instant, the end of the whip wrapped around Malik's neck, choking him. He took one hand off the reins and desperately tried to break free. Destiny was flying along at full gallop with Fahd's horse not far behind. Malik felt a jolt as he was catapulted out of the saddle and was sent flying through the air, hitting the hard ground with a thud.

The next thing he remembered was cool water on his face and voices.

"Malik, are you alright," he heard a voice ask recognising it as his father's. Slowly, he came round.

"What happened?" asked Malik. "Destiny, where is Destiny?"

"Don't worry she is okay. That evil Fahd hit you with his whip and pulled you off the horse.

"Has he been disqualified?" asked Malik, getting up to his feet and looking over at the race-goers who were leaving the event.

"You are a fine rider," said a voice nearby. Malik turned around and saw the King who said: "I would welcome someone with such talent to work and ride at my stables," he said.

Malik's father told his son that Fahd had chosen Destiny as his prize for winning the race but the King had stepped in and refused because he cheated and banished him from his land.

Malik thought about how he had let his father down and if he worked at the stables he could save money so they could buy a prized mare but that would take too long. "Father, can I go?" He asked Menna.

"Of course, my son," he said.

"Can I bring Destiny too?" Malik asked the King and he nodded.

After the King had left, Buraq approached Malik. "I saw what happened. Don't be discouraged. You have a talent. Come both of you and and have some refreshment," he said leading them to his tent.

Inside the tent as Buraq served tea, he said: "You have returned Ramsez to us. This is the second time we are in your debt. How can you we repay you?" he asked.

"I rode in the race to win the prized mare for my father and now he has nothing," said Malik, feeling a sense of sadness. "I am to work at the King's stables and that has brought me great joy and yet ... my family."

"Your father can have the choice of my mares," said Buraq. Malik's eyes lit up and he beamed a huge smile.

"Thank you, Buraq." he said.

"No thank *you*, Malik," replied Buraq.

"I would like to give you something for your help as I wouldn't have been able to take part in the race without you," said Malik getting up from the red velvet cushion and walking out of the striped tent and into his own one before returning a short time later.

"This once saved my life in the sandstorm and healed Destiny when she was stabbed in the chest by the thief. I would like to give it to you to bring your people good fortune," said Malik pressing the crystal into Buraq's hand.

"Inshallah," replied Buraq, looking down at the smooth white pebble and thinking how unremarkable it looked. He understood the young man had little and it obviously meant a great deal to him. He was very grateful nonetheless.

Present Day, Jaball

"That was fascinating, Abdul, and it's great background for my article. Thank you," said Gemma smiling before alighting the vehicle.

"Let me know if you need anything else," said Abdul.

As Gemma watched the vehicle speed away from outside the newspaper office in Dubai, she wondered if the attack has anything to do with what Sharon told her about the discovery of oil in Jaball.

Gemma recalled more than a week ago, wandering around the sea of international trade stands in the massive exhibition centre in Downtown Dubai. Gemma could only think about how boring this type of job was. *How on earth am I going to get a decent angle for a story here?* she thought before reaching down into her brown leather handbag and feeling for her mobile, before looking up at the massive diamond-shaped domed ceiling. There was no doubt it was impressive. Everything about this city was just that – amazing.

"Gemma," she heard her name called and instantly recognized the voice.

"What are you doing here," said Gemma turning around to look at her pal Sharon.

"You know me, any port in a storm," she chuckled, thinking about her next client and what needed to be done. "Look, I shouldn't be saying this but you're my pal and I trust you," said Sharon beckoning Gemma over towards the buffet table.

"I've got a tip," she said.

"Tip?" replied Gemma.

"I've heard there's a move to drill for oil here," said Sharon eyeing up the mouth-watering food with an ice sculpture of a bird as the centre-piece.

"So, what's unusual about that," Gemma replied raising her blonde eyebrows while looking over at the Italian delegation gathering around one of the trade stands.

"It's in Jaball," said Sharon.

"It can't be," replied Gemma.

"It is!" insisted Sharon. Gemma had been there with Abdul. It was a combination of modern buildings integrated with traditional Arabian architecture. *Who would even consider drilling for oil in a city centre*? Gemma pondered.

He was so passionate about his land and his people. It was evident from the way he spoke so convincingly about his life. Gemma knew how important Jaball was to Abdul, to his people, his heritage.

"So, what's this all about oil," asked Gemma looking out of one of the huge square shaped windows to the rows of palm trees swaying hypnotizing in the soft sea breeze.

"One of my snitches told me oil has been discovered in Jaball," said Sharon.

"But how do you know that's true?" asked Gemma.

"I know. He sent me a video. I saw the whole thing. Here let me show you," said Sharon reaching into her powder blue suede handbag before rummaging around and pulling out her hand. Opening her palm she turned to Gemma. "Here, see for yourself," she said placing the pen drive in Gemma's outstretched hand.

Gemma brought out her laptop and inserted the drive into the machine. What she saw unnerved her. How could this possibly be happening? Surely there are bylaws to protect people and their heritage from such exploitation?

"Why would someone be so indifferent and dismissive of the possibility of danger to the people and the environment that may be irreparable?" Gemma asked Sharon.

"The region is under great pressure from the industry and Western influences. That kind of potential wealth makes people mad, so someone is desperate," she replied.

"Okay, but Qamar has oil rigs in the north of the country. Why not just drill more there? Gemma asked, rhetorically. "I think we need to know more about who's behind this. So let's do something about this, like find out *whoever* may be responsible," said Gemma.

"You know it's not going to be easy. We're talking big money and powerful people with unlimited resources at their fingertips. I want to get them as bad as you do but you need to know what you're facing. It could get dangerous, hell yes! it will probably be very dangerous.

These types don't mess around. I know from experience," said Sharon, thinking back to her days as a police inspector in Glasgow, Scotland.

Chapter Three

Qamar State, the Evening before the King's Departure - The King's Study

Aquil sat in his ornate lounge office and looked over at the painting of a peregrine falcon. He felt pleased with himself. Arrangements had been made and if all went well the King would no longer be a problem with his ambitions. Striding over to the bird, his long white robe billowing out behind him, he took the work of art with both hands, moving it slightly to one side to reveal a peephole into King Aariz's private study. Despite modern surveillance methods, he preferred the old ways best.

Placing his narrow screwed-up coal-black eye over the hole he saw a curved object mounted on a piece of wood perched on the chest of drawers near the large table. The deadly Scimitar sword, its ornate curved blade so sharp it could cut a silk handkerchief in half, had belonged to his father, a military leader who led a coup against the King but he was killed in the bloody attack.

Aquil was only a boy at the time but he could never forgive the King for the loss of his father and vowed vengeance. He used deception to gain position within the palace security service and through time managed to rise to the position of head of security, responsible for protecting the two princes Abdul and Khalid. The King grew to trust him over the years and appointed him as his adviser, a position of great trust.

Over the years Aquil tainted Khalid's mind against his brother, Abdul, with the one single goal of ensuring Khalid became ruler of Qamar and, thereby, Aquil could exert more power and control over the Kingdom.

Aquil always suspected that King Aariz had links to an ancient tribe and had been hiding artefacts but he couldn't find out where which was an increasing frustration over the years. He must find something to discredit the King.

As time moved on his patience was wearing thin so he decided to bore a hole in the wall next door to secretly observe what His Highness was up to. He waited patiently for King Aariz to attend to business at his desk before getting up from the chair and going over to his father's sword which was made out of the finest Damascus steel, watching as the King pulled out a top drawer and pressed his fingers on the wood.

The sword was framed in a glass case mounted on a wooden plinth with elaborate engravings on a silver band wrapped around it. King Aariz flipped the plinth over, put his hand into the hole, and brought out a sepia-coloured parchment bound with a red ribbon and then pressed the same spot bringing the sword back down.

Aquil grinned but he would bide his time and pick the right moment when the King was away on royal business so he wouldn't be disturbed.

A few hours later, when the King had retired Aquil went into the study and walked over to his father's sword and repeated the same steps the King had carried out. His anticipation heightened at the thought of what the parchment may reveal and carefully undid the ribbon, slowly unfurling the paper.

He recognised the ancient hieroglyphics as the King had taught them to Abdul and Khalid as boys and Aquil was an avid intelligent scholar. He looked at the strange symbols and began to translate, his gold pen working overtime as he became increasingly excited at what he was discovering.

After a while he put the pen down clasping his hands together and leaning them on his bearded chin, his coal black eyes narrowing as he took in the enormity of what he had deciphered. He unclasped his hand, rolled up the scroll, tied the ribbon and placed it back in the hole in the desk, repeating the same procedure.

Slowly walking out of the study and closing the door behind him, he began to search for Khalid to plot his next move.

Khalid was taking his father's latest toy out for a spin — a red Lamborghini Veneno Roadster. Khalid knew his father would be furious if he found out he was driving it but, so what, he was bored. His father was an avid racing car fan and this was the jewel in his stable full of expensive models.

As he pushed the accelerator pedal further into the floor, the car took off, gaining speed with every second.

Turning the sharp corner tightly, Khalid suddenly realised he was running out of road. He tried to counter-balance but it was too late and the car spun off the road, bouncing off a safety barrier and then back on the road again to the screeching of brakes and acrid smell of burning tyres.

Finally, Khalid managed to bring the car to a halt and breathed deeply. He was okay but what about the car? Stepping out of the vehicle he walked around to the other side and winced as he saw the damage, knowing it would take more than just a paint job to fix and it had to be done before his father found out.

Driving back to the palace he contemplated his father's reaction if, and when, he found out and shrugged his shoulders. What was the worst he could do to him? He remembered how furious his father was when he returned home unexpectedly after being expelled from boarding school in England for drinking alcohol in the dorm with a few pupils.

Abdul was his favourite son and always had been. Their mother had died in childbirth 'from complications' he had told them as young boys.

Khalid believed he was second-best and he resented Abdul, who was smart and popular, while he remained introvert and friendless, despite Abdul's efforts to include him in all their activities throughout their childhood.

Over the years the resentment had been fuelled by Aquil, who wanted Khalid to be the ruler so he could bask in the power and glory and exert his control over the young Prince.

Pulling into the vast garage and parking between an Aston Martin CC100 Speedster Concept and pewter-coloured Rolls Royce Phantom, Khalid took out his mobile phone and dialled a number.

"I need to see you and quickly," he said in Arabic, "Meet me at the garage straight away," he barked ending the call.

Fifteen minutes later Aquil arrived in a white Mercedes, parked and walked over to Khalid.

"What kept you so long?" snapped Khalid.

"I have good news, my Prince," said Aquil, looking at the damaged vehicle.

"Well, I hope it is better than mine," said Khalid.

Aquil surveyed the damage. "I will take care of this," he said, knowing a custom bodywork garage worker he could bribe to do the job and compel to keep silent.

"Good!" replied Khalid. "Have it uplifted immediately and the work done in short time, but before my father's return," he said. Aquil nodded his willingness. As Aquil walked away a few steps, Khalid suddenly remembered. "What is this good news you have to tell me?" asked Khalid feeling more optimistic now it looked like he was off the hook.

"I have discovered some interesting news, my Prince; information that will be valuable to us both and for Qamar," teased Aquil.

"I see, once you have settled this business come to my quarters and we will discuss it further," commanded Khalid.

"You will not be disappointed," promised Aquil as he watched Khalid take the keys for the silver Porche 918 Spyder Concept, jump in and speed off. Boys with their toys, he sighed, looking through the contact on his mobile phone for the garage worker's number, and wondering how he was going to fob the King off with an excuse about the car if he spotted it missing.

After making arrangements to repair the damaged car, Aquil left the garage and drove to Khalid's quarters. Once inside he told Khalid about the scroll and what he had discovered.

"This crystal is the key to the throne for you, my Prince," said Aquil. "And I now know who has it," he said smiling smugly to himself.

"Who?" demanded Khalid, taking a puff from a *hokkah* pipe, savouring the sweet, aromatic taste and handing it to Aquil, who changed the *nosil* before sucking on the end of it. He didn't like this particular flavour but he knew it would be insulting to refuse.

"It is Abdul's friend, the golden one," said Aquil, looking at Khalid's puzzled expression. "The journalist from the Chronicle who came to interview your father in the jet," added Aquil.

"Ah, yes. I remember now. We had tried to put a stop to that but my brother won, as usual," said Khalid. "But how do you know she has the crystal?" he asked.

"When we were having lunch she told us she was born with a 'hallihoo' over her head."

"Hallihoo?" replied Khalid.

"Yes, I know it is a strange word but that is what she said and in the scroll the legend says a girl born with a sacred veil over her face from an ancient tribe from the north will deliver the crystal back to its home in the crystal cave. The crystal has great powers. It gives men great strength and courage. Together we will become rich and powerful and answerable to no man," said Aquil.

"How do you know she is from the north?" he enquired.

"Because she said she was descended from the Danes and they were Vikings," replied Aquil.

"I see. So what are we going to do?" asked Khalid, his eyes lighting up in anticipation at the answer.

"We must capture her and seize the crystal," said Aquil rubbing his hands together.

"Arrange it. Now go I do not wish to be disturbed." ordered Khalid. After a short pause Khalid said: "Wait. What about our other project?"

Aquil smiled: "We have been in talks with our western backers and are proceeding as planned. When we are ready they will move in quickly and work will begin instantly. There will be no obstruction. The necessary legal documents need only your signature, Your Highness. The media have been silenced."

Khalid had a thought. "What about my brother? He ventured.

"Aquil replied: "When you are King his opinion will not matter."

"Very well Aquil, see to the car."

"Yes, my Prince," replied Aquil, bowing his head and smiling to himself walking slowly backwards out of the room.

Sharon's Apartment

Gemma was seated in the apartment she shared with Sharon waiting for her call with her odd cousin Sparks.

Although he was a little odd - some would say obsessed - he was the only one who didn't seem to notice or care.

In front of her on the table sat a parcel that was delivered three hours earlier. Gemma had signed for it and unpacked several items. Her cousin was thirty-years-old, (thirty years young he would suggest) and had left Scotland after studying Computer Science.

Sparks -real name Rhuari - acquired his nickname for his experiments - some would argue adventures - with electrical theory he had tried to put into practice. Intelligent and innovative he never seemed satisfied with just getting a positive result alone. After electronics he indulged himself in modern communications, which enabled him to utilize his other skills to pioneer components and make a lot of money. Not that that was ever his main motivation.

However, it did allow him to extend his interests into other areas. He and his staff (his 'family') had grown considerably over the years and he now operated from an unlikely district in an industrial area in New York City.

From the outside the red-bricked building was quite unspectacular, but inside the large, three-storey building had open-plan arrangement areas in which the staff carried out their designated disciplines. Sparks recruited only the best and paid well.

But money, although practical, was not really a consideration for these additions to his family, as they were all the most driven, forward thinking individuals in their particular disciplines. Sparks didn't order them or manage them. He *challenged* them.

Rumour had it that whether the FBI had wanted to access an Apple device belonging to a suspect, it was Sparks they came to for help. His success brought a hefty pay-day.

Exactly on time 'Sparks' appeared, not actually in person but for the most part in perceived person. Gemma was stunned. The device on the table activated and a projection of Sparks appeared before her eyes. The device looked to all intent and purposes like an ordinary tablet about seven inches in length and was larger than say, a cell phone but smaller than an Apple device. It was this device that projected his manifestation, but there was more. There seemed to be depth or solidity Gemma thought. "That's the kind of reaction I was expecting," he said.

"Sparks," Gemma cried, "What am I looking at?"

He responded: "You read the information I sent you? And you still are surprised?"

"No, I mean yes! You oddball, I could have been in the shower!" she replied.

Sparks' just shrugged and said: "Don't worry, the device is waterproof!"

'Sparks' projection was dressed in boxer shorts, a bath robe and socks and moccasins. He was eating what appeared to be cereal from a large plastic bowl.

"Why are you dressed like that and what are you eating?" Gemma inquired.

"Well it's morning here," he offered casually, by way of explanation. "I felt I should offer some emphasis on the gifts you didn't thank me for yet."

On the defensive, Gemma replied: "Yes, sorry, thank you very much. You're most thoughtful."

"I'll be brief," he said. "You've read the information, so I'll point out the important stuff. The device I'm looking at you from is a very special experimental device. The device itself and the others are proprietary and the technology belongs to me. I am making them available to you as my favourite test subject!

"Never, repeat, never! Turn on the device using the familiar on-off button on the side. Inside the device are two vials of acid that will activate and destroy the hard drive and processor respectively. The device is voice-activated and to start to use it you say, 'Robson, wake up!' And he will ask you your password."

"Who's Robson?" asked Gemma.

"Robson is the device butler, to help in times of trouble. Treat him nice and he will do all he can," replied Sparks.

"What if I lose my voice or I am kidnapped and gagged?" Gemma asked.

"I wish I had time for a social life. I really do," Sparks teased. "There is a sixty-four thousand (64K) megapixel camera on the front and back, but they are more than just cameras. If you do find yourself in that unlikely predicament you described, as long as you can make eye contact with one of the cameras -it doesn't matter which one - the lens will automatically read your biometric imprint of your retina and Robson will appear and ask you preset questions. Because you have not voice-activated the device he will give you options, which you will answer using blinks, one for yes and two for no - pretty standard binary options," he explained.

"I am curious about the software installed as there are some things I didn't recognize?" said Gemma.

"To all uneducated eyes the device just looks like an ordinary tablet," Sparks responded. "But it's more than that, much more. For instance, look at me now. This projection is multi-dimensional. I look like I am in the room with you. This is five dimensions, 5D," said Sparks.

"That's one of the software programmes I did not recognise," said Gemma.

"Tell Robson, 'Robson 5D' and he will open it for you. You can if you wish, touch-screen others in camera view and they will appear too. You effectively project your own and others' images as if they were you sitting together for example. There are two more programmes I am particularly proud of, Divinity and ICU. Divinity sounds religious and boring, but it is really exciting. It is software that allows the device to scan for hidden objects such as power cables, water pipes or passages. ICU is probably handier still.

"By activating ICU (I See You) one can scan for hidden cameras or recording devices, wireless points and infrared signatures. Do you see the little object that looks like a compass you plug in?" he asked. Gemma picked it up and plugged it in the device without waiting to be told.

Sparks continued: "It actually is a functional compass with a luminous option for night use. But when used with ICU it indicates where the device is!"

"I noticed there wasn't a charger in the box?" Gemma asked.

"Well spotted!" replied Sparks. "The folding magnetic cover for the screen, the dark bars? They are actually, solar panels. They charge the device and can be used as a power-bank to charge other devices."

Gemma thought for a moment before commenting "The case looks pretty standard, at least?"

"Oh you tease!" Sparks said. "Nothing is as it seems. We made the case out of titanium; you could literally have an elephant stand on it and it would not affect the operation of the device."

"You could just say it's tough instead of all that elaborate description, "Gemma replied.

Sparks paused for a moment. He said: "No, I couldn't. I mean it. We actually had an elephant stand on it!"

"Have you seen the hairbrush for your pretty hair," he asked?

Gemma picked it up. "How thoughtful," she said.

Sparks asked: "Turn the handle away from you and operate the catch."

Gemma did so and was startled to see a four-inch spike shoot out of the handle. "That's pretty urgent," she cried turning the handle to see the spike inside the handle and noticing that the spike was serrated on one side.

Sparks continued: "The back of the brush head, the round motif? It is a tracker. If you open the brush head at the back you can see a mirror and on the opposite side a solar panel. This feeds the tracker with power so that it never runs down and you can also use the device as a power bank too." Gemma was amazed.

"You have really outdone yourself this time," she said.

"I have to keep an eye on my little Cuz and make sure she is OK in this wild and unpredictable world," he replied.

"You always do, ever since I was very small," said Gemma. "I am really appreciative, I really am." He looked a little embarrassed.

"Look you've probably had a long day so, let's leave it there and I'll be watching! Bye," said Sparks and like that, he was gone. Later that evening while in bed, Gemma re-read the information that Sparks had sent to her mobile. She was amazed to find she had access with her mobile and device to satellites and the information was encrypted.

As an added feature, Gemma learned that if anyone was able to decrypt the data it wouldn't really help them. When decrypted, the data was in Arapahoe language. *Dear Sparks,* thought Gemma. *He really did think of everything*! There was even a Velcro carrier and strap for her arm or leg.

Chapter Four

Qamar Gold Cup

Gemma had become a regular visitor at the Royal Stables as she researched her article on the King and his racing dynasty. She had managed to persuade Wullie for more time to include a piece on the Qamar Gold Cup and with the lure of 'world exclusive' his ego was so big he couldn't resist.

Blossom had run an excellent time on the gallops earlier that morning. Stable boy Nylah was a talented jockey, the gift running through the generations going back to the days when Malik took part in the Bedouin horse race on his mare Destiny. The story of the legendary race had been recited through the generations.

Abdul had been training Blossom for the cup since she was a yearling. Her sire was Dancer and Abdul would never forget the moment he saw the black stallion.

He was working at his father's stables and had been out riding when he heard what sounded like whinnies and thumping. He couldn't quite make out the sounds but rode over in the direction of the noise. Then he saw a sight which made him sick to the pit of his stomach. There in front of him was a man standing beating a horse tied to a tree with a stick.

Abdul quickly jumped off his grey horse. He could feel his blood boiling and ran over to the man. Grabbing the piece of wood Abdul battered him with it. The man looked into Abdul's bulging red eyes and fled for his life.

Abdul turned to the poor creature, the blood oozing from its wounds. He approached gently, very gently, talking quietly, soothingly. The relationship began and would never end. Even now Dancer would only let Abdul ride him.

Blossom was the biggest challenge he had come across. She was pure as the driven snow, a proud Arabian, strong yet supple and had breeding lines believed to be from Alexander the Great's magnificent steed Bucephalus, all those centuries ago. But she was also stubborn as a mule.

The bloodline at the royal stables was kept pure from the time Malik arrived with Destiny. Malik's descendants all worked for the various Kings over the years and life was good. Abdul was particularly proud of Destiny's Child, a descendant of Destiny. He thought she would be a good match with his stallion Dancer.

Abdul remembered the morning Blossom was born. Nylah and Abdul had been working a young colt in the arena early one morning before the sun came up.

"What do you think about Destiny's Child and Dancer? Do you think they would a perfect match to throw a foal?"

Nylah thought a while and recalled the story of his ancestor Malik in the Bedouin horse race. How I would love to race, he thought. "Yes, it would be good," replied the young boy.

However, the courtship between the two was less than perfect when it came to the time to cover Destiny's Child and Dancer narrowly escaped a good kicking during the process but it was a trouble-free pregnancy and Abdul and Nylah took it in turns during the nights to be with the mare when it was nearing time for the birth.

One night Nylah had fallen asleep in the hay in the stable and when he awoke got the surprise of his life - a lovely foal suckling from his mum. He watched in awe at the perfect creature and doting, proud look on the mare's face.

Slowly walking up to touch Destiny's Child's face, he whispered: "Well done, my beauty," he said stroking the base of her ears which she loved. After examining the foal and determining it was a filly, he pondered what to call her.

"What shall we call her?" asked Nylah.

Abdul's mind drifted to an image in his father's garden in the palace. He could smell the sweet flower which brought home boyhood memories playing with his twin brother Khalid. His father had brought seeds back from his trip abroad to grow in the garden. "We'll call her Blossom - Apple Blossom," said Abdul.

And so in time the young filly's training began and Abdul's patience would be tested to the limit. He tried to get through to Blossom but she was having none of it. He knew he had to gain her respect or there would be no progress. She was a highly talented, spirited little mare who was sharp.

Abdul knew he would have to have a breakthrough before he could back her and remembered his father, who was also a natural horseman, telling him: 'Go back to basics'.

He took the rope halter and put it over Blossom's pert snowy white head and clipped on a 20ft lead rope. He backed her up by putting pressure on her nose and she immediately reared up and tried to spin in mid-air and break free but Abdul was too quick. She came back down and Abdul repeated the exercise until, after what seemed like an age, Blossom stood still. Abdul tweaked the rope to beckon her forward and she stubbornly planted four legs on the ground and refused to budge.

It'll take as long as it takes, thought Abdul as he watched Blossom tilt her head to one side and curl her lip as she tried to work out what to do. If she takes a step forward, that's it, thought Abdul to himself and he watched as she took the first step.

Abdul reached up and stroked her nose and she nestled it into his hand. It was a special moment and the bond had begun. The months rolled on and Blossom was growing stronger and more powerful with every passing season and Abdul was impressed with her training, although she could still have the odd temper tantrum and was known in the yard as a bit of a diva.

But Abdul and Nylah persevered and worked hard for the Qamar Gold Cup which attracted only the *'creme de la creme'* of race horses from all over the land.

Abdul thought back to the time when Gemma had visited the stables and he had pretended to be a stable groom but she had forgiven him for teasing her and Gemma's deep love of horses was a perfect match for Abdul's passion and together they prepared Blossom for the event of the year.

Gemma also found the filly wilful and cheeky but it was hard to be cross with her as she had a soft, kind eye and could turn on the charm when she wanted. Blossom was born to be a champion as her Arabian bloodline was the best in the world.

"The Arabian is built for speed and endurance and was considered a sacred creature, a gift from Allah, legend has it," Abdul told her one day while they were discussing Blossom's training schedule with Nylah.

"The convex forehead is believed to carry blessings, while its arched neck and high crest is a sign of courage and a high tail represents pride," he said.

"Well, she certainly has plenty of that," replied Gemma, watching Blossom bolt full pelt round the lush green field, pausing to buck and then rear before finally crouching down on all fours and having a roll. She then got up, shook herself down, before bending down to eat the grass which was specially cultivated in the searing heat. All the stables were air-conditioned and no expense was spared on the caring for King Aariz's world-class, prize-winning equestrian stock.

Gemma marvelled at the mass of green grass against the golden sand surrounding the stables - it was an oasis in an otherwise desert environment.

Abdul, Nylah and Gemma were all excited about the race. Soon the day had arrived and the excitement was building at the racetrack in the outskirts of Jaball. The horses and their jockeys had lined up at the start of the race and seconds later, they were off!

The thunder of the galloping hooves pounding on the turf was unmistakable as the jockeys in their brightly-coloured silks bunched up hugging the white railings as they raced around the track in the biggest, richest and most prestigious horse race in the world.

It was undoubtedly the event of the year and all the movers and shakers were there.

The field were turning round for the last lap and home. Gemma could see Blossom tucked in behind a chestnut horse. She was following the jockey's blue and gold colours intently and couldn't keep her eyes off the group which had now strung out after an exhausting pace. It could be a lap record but that was of no concern. Now all she could think about was Blossom."Come on, come on," shouted Gemma at the top of her voice. "You can do it," yelled Gemma, almost hoarse from shouting.

The field were turning for the home straight, clumps of turf flew through the air as the horses galloped full pelt, the tension mounting - all eyes were on the front runners. The 'chestnut' was ahead by a couple of lengths and gaining more distance away from Blossom. The noise from the crowd intensified as it reached fever pitch. "Blossom, it's Blossom," shouted Abdul. "She's catching up. Go, go," he yelled as he watched the filly gain valuable ground on the 'chestnut'.

The winning post was coming up fast. All Abdul's hopes and dreams of breeding a winner were on the line. He had worked so hard with the stubborn little filly.

Gemma closed her eyes, clutched the brown leather pouch around her neck, squeezing the small, round hard object inside willing the little mare to win.

Suddenly, Blossom felt a surge of power flowing through her whole body. Her heart began to beat even faster as the blood rushed through her veins. Her strike lengthened and quickened. The turf kicked up behind her as she motored on head-to-head with the chestnut. It was stride-for-stride as the line drew nearer, the noise of the crowd was deafening as the winning post was only a few feet away. Summoning up all her strength and determination, Nylah urged Blossom on and she struck out careering over the line to victory sending the crowd into frenzy.

"She won, she won," cried Abdul, raising his hands in triumph. He was panting with excitement as if he had run the race himself. "Right, let's go to the winner's enclosure." Abdul and Gemma fought their way through the tight crowd to the enclosure where Nylah had just dismounted and was carrying his saddle into the weighing room.

As Abdul approached the filly, Blossom nickered and instinctively he threw his arms around her strong, sweaty, muscled neck and she nuzzled into him.

"I am so proud of you, my girl," Abdul beamed as Gemma stroked her nose and kissed her.

Abdul's father and other dignitaries approached offering their congratulations and Blossom took all the fuss in her stride.

Congratulating Abdul and Nylah, King Aariz said: "You have done well. She is a fine filly who will no doubt produce the finest offspring and continue the tradition of our pure bloodlines," and then, after a short speech, he presented Abdul with the Qamar Gold Cup to the resounding cheers from the crowd.

Later, while enjoying a meal at a local restaurant, Gemma reflected over the day's excitement. "Your father mentioned the pure bloodline. Why is that so important to you?"

"It is everything. Legend has it that the Arabian is a gift from Allah. For centuries my people have bred from only the purest bloodline. To dedicate themselves, ourselves to this ideal, is to show gratitude and honour him. My father and his father can recite the best war mares' bloodline for centuries. It is the Bedouin way and is passed down from generation to generation."

Gemma fingered the pouch around her neck remembering the time she first saw the smooth white pebble in a pool of water while walking in the hills near her home in Scotland.

Dumyat, Stirling, Scotland – Three Months Earlier

"You know an ancient tribe called the Maeatae used to live here centuries ago, actually a confederation of tribes fleeing the Roman world," said a strong male voice. It was snowy and cold. Gemma shivered as she pulled up the collar of her heavy green waterproof jacket.

Tiny snowflakes began falling down onto her old black French beret and she was glad she had stuck it in her rucksack at the last minute before the climb up Dumyat, in the Ochils in Stirling. Heather carpeted the sides of the hill and popped up intermittently through the snow as Gemma took small steps up the steep, southern part of the hill. Duncan was striding as if it was race against time but he was used to it, an ex-paratrooper, who didn't suffer fools gladly, he bounded up the hill.

The south-east side of the hill was practically vertical. No one in their right mind assailed Dumyat from this side, most directly. "I need a breather," shouted Gemma.

We'll stop just below the top," replied Duncan. Gemma felt a chill. Duncan noticed and advised she put her spare fleece on over her jacket, at least until they set off again. Even though it was cold, her face was red with exertion, the surge of energy needed to tread through the snow, taking care not to slip or fall. It was like walking up a steep staircase with no banister. Her legs filled up with lactic acid, feeling more like battery acid.

"Okay, we'll stop for five," said Duncan, taking off his huge, green camouflaged pack which must have weighed at least fifty pounds. He reached inside the side pocket for a black plastic water container and handed it to Gemma who was looking up at the piercing blue clear sky.

There was not one single cloud. It was a perfect day with fantastic panoramic views over to Edinburgh, Fife and the Forth Valley. Looking northwest, she could see Ben Ledi, another favourite hill of Gemma's, though the last memory was not her favourite, being caught in a whiteout at the top of the Munro.

"The Maeatae called Dumyat their sacred hill," said Duncan opening a bar of chocolate and offering a piece to Gemma.

"Sacred?" asked Gemma, popping the square piece of chocolate into her dry mouth savouring its sweet release.

"Yes. Dumyat (*Dun Mhead*) is thought to originate from Dun (hill fort) of the Maeatae. Over to your right you can still see the marks in the ground where the wooden fort was built. Gemma turned her head and glanced over to the flat area Duncan had indicated, just making out the outlines where the structure probably once stood.

"They fought the Roman army right here in this area, he said waving his hand over the valley. Not a particularly large tribe in itself, the Maeatae had swelled their ranks from other tribes such as the *Iceni, Votadini* and *Brigante.* These tribes and others had fled imperialism and went where they hoped the invaders would not follow. If these hills could talk, just think about what secrets they would reveal," he continued.

"How long ago was that?" she asked.

"Oh about 180-200AD," Duncan replied. "Didn't you know that some people are convinced all mountains are holy places?" he asked her before getting up and swinging his heavy rucksack onto one shoulder, "because they bring us closer to God."

Oddly enough, Gemma had never heard Duncan speak about any god before. He continued as Gemma prepared herself by removing her fleece. "You know you are not doing so badly. All through our time together you have applied yourself and I've seen the change in you."

At her father's request, Duncan, his good friend, had taken Gemma under his wing and set about preparing her for the rigours of life as he thought. He had seen to it that she had enrolled in a self-defence course and stuck to it. He had taken her on many road runs, he called Tabbing - (Tactical Advance to Battle) after a month she could battle-march ten miles with a thirty-pound pack in two hours.

Now he was continuing her introduction to hills. They had been on many hikes together, to and up the many Munros' spread all over Scotland. (A Munroe is a mountain of over three thousand feet or 914.4 metres). In addition, Duncan had taught Gemma outdoor survival skills including tracking game animals and field-craft. Duncan had promised today's outing would be a short one - about eight miles, with the 'hard part' first. He looked at Gemma. "You know there are some things that I won't be able to teach you fully," said Duncan.

"Like what? Gemma asked.

"Mental toughness and biological equation," he said. "Mental toughness is something you have to learn by yourself but you have developed that to a degree already," he said. "Get your map and compass out and I'll give you the next destination." When she had done this he gave her a six-figure map reference. "Show me where we are and where we are headed," he directed.

Gemma did so. "Bearing and route?" said Duncan. When Gemma did this and apparently satisfied, Duncan added: "OK, take us there."

They moved off Dumyat Hill with Gemma leading the way, and after they had gone a short distance Gemma called over her right shoulder: "What do you mean by biological equation?"

"Every creature on this planet, people included, have to weigh up the risks or rewards in life. If they get it right they thrive, if they don't they lose, usually with their life. So it's important to get it right. You will have to make choices and recognize opportunities. Every creature, predator or prey has to do this."

Hang on, thought Gemma: "I'm only going to Dubai Duncan, not the jungle!" said Gemma.

He was quick with his answer and emphasis: "Anywhere there are people you *are* in a jungle and don't forget it. People kill more people every year on this planet by wars, accidents, stupidity or malice. Look what people have done to the earth. They are toxic."

Gemma was a little surprised at the force with which he made his point. "There are good people too," she said.

"Too much talking, not enough walking," he countered. He usually said 'If you have breath to talk, you can walk!'

As they approached their destination, in this case the Battle of Sheriffmuir memorial, they stopped at the Wharry Burn. Gemma removed her pack and took out her water bottle. As she bent down to fill it she noticed something sparkle in the water. At first she thought she imagined it but it glinted again. She paused when she reached for it, thinking it may be glass. The hypnotic effect of the water flowing partially obscured the object. It was a strange shape, partially hidden behind a dark grey stone. It seemed clear, like glass and yet had shape to it.

Gemma was curious. What could it be? Inspecting it closer she thought she could see what she thought was a crystal. And yet, there was shape. Was it an angel? Wings certainly, but the body seemed more horse-like. Yes, a horse with wings! Intrigued, she took a step nearer, removed her warm black woollen right glove and dipped her hand into the freezing cold stream, shivering as the icy liquid soaked through her skin.

Just as she touched the crystal a flashing beam of light burst up into the sky knocking her to the ground. Staring up in amazement and wonder, there unfolding in around her was something surreal.

Bare-chested men with long straggly hair, their bodies and faces covered with blue tattoos of birds and strange images, were racing in chariots, hurling axes, spears and rounded stones charging towards an army of men who were clad in armour. The warriors were waving their spears and rattling the bronze apple attached to the end of the spear shaft.

Gemma watched as a female warrior covered in the same distinctive tattoos, her long white mane flowing out behind her chariot, gallop the pony at full speed at the strange tortoise-shaped formation of soldiers. The shrieking sounds and blood-curdling noises from the tribesmen riding in their horse-drawn chariots sounded terrifying.

Her name was Eithne, a fearless Maeatae warrior, the daughter of the tribe's chieftain Argentcoccus, a match for any of her peers, and never yielded no matter what her predicament. Their very existence depended on it. The Romans and her father had signed a peace treaty but time had proved Roman words meant nothing. The Maeatae and other tribes wanted peace and freedom so had joined forces with the *Caledonii*, a powerful tribe from the north, to strengthen numbers against the mighty Roman invaders.

The warriors had chosen to attack a pathway the enemy had to use. It was bordered on both sides with swamp and they had prepared well. Eithne and her fellow warriors had been submerged up to their necks, with only their heads showing, in a cold, foul bog for two days with only a few berries and a high-energy gum they had prepared to fortify them. They lay patiently in ambush, hidden and waiting for their enemy to show.

Gemma saw the enemy approaching as Eithne jumped out of the bog and into her chariot to join the surprise attack. But just as she was gaining momentum galloping towards the Roman army her chariot hit a rock propelling Eithne up through the air like an acrobat, twisting and turning, before falling down and hitting the soft earth below.

Eithne was lying spread-eagled on the ground. Gemma heard the terrifying screams of dying men and smelt the acrid odour of death, a sickening feeling swirled around her stomach. She watched as Eithne turned her head to the right and looked at a pair of brown woollen socks encased by a pair of battered leather sandals.

What happened next filled Gemma with fear and trepidation. She heard the chink of steel grey metal armour and heard a voice shouting in Latin. Suddenly a soldier with a red plume sticking out of his helmet stood above Eithne, raised his bloodied sword high above his head with both hands preparing for a downward thrust. Summoning up all her might Gemma watched as Eithne raised her right leg and kicked him between the legs, as he cried out in agony and fell to the ground.

Eithne was then grabbed and dragged along the wet grass for several minutes before stopping behind a large rock. Looking up she saw a man with long brown shoulder-length hair, with a plait, tied at the end with a strip of brown leather, hang down either side of his face.

Gemma heard him say "Are you hurt? Can you sit up?" Slowly Eithne began to move and a hand helped her to a sitting position. "We better get back to cover. It's not safe here," he said holding out his strong-looking square-shaped hand. Eithne grasped it and the pair disappeared into the wooded area emerging breathless, a short time later at a large wooden fort at the summit of the crag.

The white mist had covered most of the tall structure with only the tops of the ramparts peeping through. It was guarded by tattooed-covered sentries at their posts. The fortress was the only break in the thick, dense forest which was well protected by the steep cliffs and gulley. The view over the land was spectacular and a superb vantage point where the warriors could see their enemies from afar.

Walking up to the familiar structure the couple approached the sentries who opened the large, heavy wooden double doors allowing the wafting putrid smells of raw sewage to escape as the pair entered the vast enclosure.

As Eithne walked through the thick brown mud, people began to emerge from the wooden structures topped with thatch or peat.

Gemma watched as the couple stopped at a hut, which was considerably larger than the rest. Eithne spoke to the two guards who stepped aside to let them in. The man followed behind examining the blue tattoos of animals, a wolf, snake and eagle, surrounding a large winged horse in the centre of her slender but strong back.

Sitting beside the fire in the centre of the dwelling was a man with long grey straggly hair and a beard, bare-chested and with similar tattoos etched on his skin.

He looked up and Eithne stared into his piercing pale blue eyes, noticing a deep scar over his left eye which continued down his narrow cheekbone finishing at the end of his curled lip.

"Was the attack a success?" Gemma heard him ask and watched as the chieftain continued polishing the point of a spear on the end of a wooden pole.

"Yes, father but we lost many warriors," replied Eithne. Argentcoccus stood up, his silver shin-guards and single strip of metal around his neck and waist reflecting in the red and amber glow of the fire's flames. "Success has many fathers' but defeat is an orphan," he offered.

"Who is this man at your side?" asked Argentcoccus.

"He saved my life, father," replied Ethine.

"My name is Cinoid, of the *Caledonii*," he said.

"Mmm," Argentcoccus replied, beckoning them both to sit down and motioning them to join him. Fish, berries and water was available from brown wooden bowls. Ethine was starving as she had only had eaten a local-made gum used by warriors for energy, during the days spent waiting in the swamp, but she had no appetite.

Argentcoccus bent his head and looked down at his silver shin-guards which had been formed from melted down silver coins given as a bribe by the Romans to keep the peace and he was beginning to feel guilty.

"The taxes on my people are too high. These Romans are ordering us to worship their Emperor and taking our sons away to fight for them in foreign lands. We need to plan more attacks and drive them from our land," he said angrily. If our young men and women must fight it should be for us and all our futures. We must make plans. Eithne will take you to a shelter where you can rest and we will discuss more at length at sunrise ... Thank you for helping my daughter."

Eithne and Cinoid stood up and left the warm glow of the fire, stepping out into the cold night air. It was a dark and ominous sky which hurried into night. A bright moon dominated the sky and the stars began to emerge around it, twinkling like far-off silver campfires.

As they passed a standing stone in the centre of the camp, Cinoid looked at the strange symbols carved into the solid grey shape. His eyes were drawn to the shape of a small horse with wings, and he remembered seeing the tattoo on Eithne's back.

"It's Pegasus, favourite winged steed of the Greek god Zeus," said Eithne, remembering her father telling his people of the time an Egyptian princess and her people were given safe haven by the Maeatea when they were chased from their lands by the Romans. She gifted the Pegasus Crystal to the tribe and we worshipped it in a secret location on the hill. The crystal's magical powers healed the sick and gave courage and strength to warriors in battle.

Gemma watched as Eithne looked at Cinoid's curious expression and then showed him to his sleeping place before returning to her father's lodge.

"I have heard that the Romans have been asking questions about that which we hold most dear. The crystal," said Argentcoccus.

"What kind of questions, father?" replied Eithne.

"The Second Legion's emblem is Pegasus and they have seen our tattoos and carvings on the great stone," he replied.

"We will never reveal the crystal to them no matter what," said Eithne feeling irritated as she did not agree with the peace deal in the first place.

"My spies tell me the Romans are torturing our people to find out where the crystal is. They have conspired with our factious neighbours and no doubt heard of its powers and will covet it for their Emperor. It will only be a matter of time before they find it and take it from us. You must take the crystal and hide it until we can defeat our enemies and it can be returned safely to our people. Our warriors will drink from the water blessed by the Pegasus Crystal before battle commences so we have great courage and strength to defeat them," he continued.

"But father, I want to defeat our enemy. I am strong. I can beat any warrior in the tribe," she protested.

"I need someone I can trust. Do you understand, daughter," he replied.

"Yes, father. I will leave at first light," said Eithne.

As they rose to take their leave, they heard the voice of the old man say, gently: "I saw her once, you know." They both turned and approached him.

"Scotia ... I saw her. I was but a boy of just eight summers when she arrived with her people. I stood on the very hill with my father and our people and wondered what we were watching. From a distance the great water that led to the sea was full of brightly coloured birds skimming over the surface of the water. But as they got closer we could see the vessels more clearly." The old man stared into the fire and continued. "Great vessels – five in all – headed up river towards us; larger than anything we had ever seen. Some people forgot their natural fear of strangers and headed down to the waterside to get a better view. They were not disappointed; great wooden vessels made of wood, carved and painted with bright colours. The people on the ships smiled and waved at them and showed no hostility but a keen readiness to be as one. Soon after through others, we were told their leaders wished to meet us and it was arranged. I was just a boy but slipped into the meet to see for myself. Their leader was a beautiful woman who came bearing a gift and was humble. She wore a tall hat that made her taller than the men present and yellow metal was hung around her neck and belt. Her eyes were painted like a beast of the forest and as I was transfixed by them but I thought she showed a deep sadness."

"What happened then?" asked Eithne.

"I was discovered and removed from the meeting, the old man said. I never found out."

The next day Eithne rose before dawn in preparation for her task ahead. She knew the path to the secret waterfall like the back of her hand but she would have to be extra careful as the Romans and their allies were ever watchful.

Steadfastly, she made her way along the muddy path until she finally reached the waterfall. Stepping behind it she walked over a pool, bent down and saw the small horse shape with wings. She scooped it up and watched as the horse disappeared to reveal a smooth white pebble. Clutching it in her hands, she turned to walk out from behind the waterfall and felt a hand on her shoulder.

She reached for the knife in her belt and in the struggle the pebble flew up into the air and down onto the ground.

"Eithne, it's me, Cinoid," said a male voice.

Eithne stopped and looked up into narrow hazel eyes and a furrowed brow. "What are you doing here?" she yelled.

"I saw you leave early and thought you may be in danger from the Romans," he replied.

"Danger? No, I am well," she insisted.

"Is this what you are looking for?" he asked, holding up the white stone. Eithne's stomach lurched. She would have to play it cool and calm. He must not suspect the crystal and everything it meant to her people.

"That, no," she replied, shrugging her shoulders.

"So you won't mind if I keep it," he said popping the stone into the brown leather belt around his waist. The look on Eithne's face said it all - fear, disappointment, loss, hopelessness.

"Look, I know about the crystal and the legend," said Cinoid.

"How do you know?" asked Eithne.

"You're not the only people who have eyes and ears, you know," he said smiling.

"We need to hide it, somewhere the Romans will never find it," said Cinoid. "Where do you hide something which is in plain sight all along?" he said with a twinkle in his eye.

Eithne stopped and thought for a while. *Where indeed?* It has to be somewhere no one would think of looking. After a few minutes her eyes lit up. "I know," she said the excitement rising in her voice.

"Come with me, Cinoid. I know the very spot," she said.

"Then you should have this," he said tossing the pouch containing the crystal to her. The pair began walking through the dense forest … they headed north approximately four miles as the crow flies. An image appeared to Gemma of an ambush attack by Roman archers and in the desperate attempt to escape, Eithne was fatally wounded. With her dying effort Eithne stretched out her arm and gave the crystal Cinoid who managed to evade the attackers and escape. *It was safe,* she thought, before she closed her eyes for the last time. Cinoid returned to his people, the Caledonii, in the far north where he and his other tribe members intermingled with through generations until spreading west they eventually encountered Christianity. Some time in their unremembered and unrecorded history they gifted the crystal to a new Christian settlement, at Iona.

Duncan asked: "Are you OK? You seemed miles away..."

Gemma tried to gather her thoughts about what had just happened. "I think I was," she replied. She felt strange, almost like having a dream when you're awake. Is such a thing possible she wondered? Not all things in life are what they seem, she conceded with the exception of Duncan, perhaps.

Gemma believed she had known him forever; her father placed great faith in Duncan, though he was younger than her father by eight years. She remembered, when younger, she had called him 'uncle' and had been encouraged by her parents to do so, but Duncan seemed bemused by the title. As Gemma grew older she just called him by his name and he seemed not to notice or care.

"If you're finished meditating let's head back," he said.

"I was trying to remember when I stopped calling you 'uncle' and started using 'Duncan' she offered.

He turned to Gemma and looked at her intently. "It doesn't matter what you call me, just that you *do* call me. Gemma, I mean it. If you ever need me anytime, anywhere, for anything, don't hesitate for one moment. I'll be annoyed if you don't." Gemma smiled her appreciation and with that brief exchange they gathered themselves and headed back down off the hills.

Chapter Five

Dubai - Secret Library

Around five-thirty in the evening the silver Aston Martin CC100 Speedster Concept pulled up outside the Desert Springs Village apartment complex off Sheik Zayed Road, Dubai. Abdul called Sharon's apartment where Gemma was staying.

He got out of the driver's seat and opened the passenger door for Gemma. She looked stunning in her long white, halter neck dress which magically wrapped its way around her slender body, complementing her light golden tan and chic bobbed-style white hair.

"Hi Gemma," Abdul said. "You look very lovely."

"Not overdressed?" asked Gemma. "Not at all," Abdul responded.

Pulling up her dress to reveal perfectly manicured fuschia pink toenails and an eye-catching lilac and diamond foot thong, Gemma crouched and stepped into the powerful car.

"Before you ask," said Abdul. "It's my father's," he said putting his foot down on the accelerator and whisking off into the warm early evening. Abdul continued: "My father has always been interested in refined cars ever since he heard their power was measured in horsepower. He has quite a rare collection and has invested money and time in acquiring these precious rarities, as a sort of investment. My brother and I used to joke we had more sports cars than roads in Qamar!"

Driving along the motorway was manic as cars switching lanes at the last minute, horns honking, Porches, Lamborghinis, old battered trucks, fighting for position as they zoomed along at breakneck speed.

"So, how was your day at the Chronicle?" asked Abdul. "Did you manage to finish the article on my father's horses?" he urged, quickly swerving to avoid an old battered truck driving on the wrong side of the carriageway.

"Hectic, as usual," replied Gemma. "We just made deadline. The feature and pictures looked great. Wullie was so mad I managed to do it," she smiled wryly remembering her news editor's face flushing as he realised just how talented a writer she was but couldn't raise the courage to tell her.

"No' bad lassie, but yiv goat a lang way tae go yet," he sneered at Gemma, who decided to ignore him. The further from you the better, she mused.

Gemma looked out of the window. The sun was getting lower on the horizon and as they sped along she asked Abdul: "What's the mystery? Where are we going?"

"I thought we would have an early meal and then visit an acquaintance of mine," he replied. As Gemma looked east ahead down the coast, she could see the outline of the unmistakable Burj-Al-Arab in the distance, the ever-growing buildings already lengthening their shadows.

They headed north on 331 Road, turning right into Al Sofouh Road. A few minutes along the D94 they turned toward the coastline and stopped outside the hotel - a unique example of architecture standing 321 metres high and fitted with gold-plated interiors. The Burj-Al-Arab (Tower of the Arabs) was immediately noticeable. The massive, sail-like hotel structure, constantly changing colours as the setting sun reflected its glory.

As they got out the car Gemma saw red, orange and yellow flames bursting from tall pillars either side of the long entrance to the hotel.

"That's some sight," said Gemma. "I understand it was built to resemble the sail of a dhow - a type of Arabian vessel - and has twenty-eight double storey floors."

"It is quite nice inside too," Abdul ventured. "Just wait till you see the restaurant. You are in for a treat."

As Gemma and Abdul walked into the magnificent hotel they were met by a team of staff who washed their hands and then poured scent into their palms before offering them a drink and sweetmeats. Gemma turned around and saw a fountain in the centre of the foyer shooting jets of water hundreds of feet into the air. As the staff left them, the pair stepped into a lift with the attendant. "Sea Restaurant," said Abdul.

"Yes, sir," replied the attendant as the glass panelled lift surged upwards and then quickly stopped. The door opened and the couple walked out into the corridor and over to a glass-fronted door trimmed with gold leaf.

They then stepped inside a yellow submarine and were whisked through a cave and into a restaurant with a massive floor-to-ceiling aquarium with sharks, rays and hundreds of small brightly-coloured fish swimming in the crystal clear turquoise blue water.

Sitting at their table Gemma looked up at the copper-coloured arch and into the eye of a passing shark. It slowed abruptly and Gemma could feel its steely-gaze penetrating her body. She shivered.

"Are you alright?" asked Abdul. "A pashmina," he said in Arabic to their personal waiter who hovered nearby.

"No, I'm fine, really," she replied before picking up a menu, gulping as she scanned down the intimidating prices.

"The Alaskan Crab is delicious and so are the Japanese scallops," said Abdul looking at Gemma who was still trying to work out the conversion rate from *Dirhams* to pounds sterling. It was a King's ransom or at least a month's salary.

"Do not worry about the cost," said Abdul, reading her mind and without looking up from the menu added: "We have a tab."

"That's a relief," she replied looking at the caviar which had a whole menu alone. Then to lighten the mood she added: "I had visions of me washing dishes here for a very long time!"

"I don't know who is on the menu, them or us," laughed Abdul watching the enormous creatures swim around the aquarium creating a hypnotic effect.

After dinner Gemma said: "That was delicious, Abdul. Thank you."

"You are very welcome. I'm glad you enjoyed it," he replied. "What is the point of nice things if you cannot share them with someone?" He added.

Excusing herself and walking towards the ladies' room she noticed how the sharks and tropical fish, which were staring at them throughout the meal, were following after her and it felt a little disconcerting. It looked odd. They remained at one end of the aquarium until she returned. And then followed her back! Nothing strange in that she thought! Just ignore the odd fish Gemma, she told herself.

The couple left the restaurant and walked a little way along the corridor to the elevator. "Leave us," he told the lift attendant who promptly did so after recognising the Prince.

"I want to show you something," said Abdul as the lift door opened and they walked inside. Moments later the lift door opened and they stepped out into the hallway. Abdul looked around and then walked over to a painting on the wall of the desert at night.

"As you know my family are Bedouins and my grandfather used to tell me stories of the desert, a place where you could live or die, where your dreams were so vivid they became reality," he said reaching up and placing his hand over a star constellation.

"Do you know what constellation it is?" asked Abdul proceeding to trace his hand around the outline of the square-shaped constellation.

"No," replied Gemma, looking inquisitively at the intriguing-looking gold-rimmed work of art. "I usually use a compass!"

"It's Pegasus. The Great Square of Pegasus is actually an asterism, meaning it is a pattern formed with a portion of the full constellation. Pegasus' brightest stars are Alpha Pegasi *or Markab,* which is the Arabic word for saddle. *Epsilon Pegasi* is the brightest star and this marks the horse's muzzle; Beta and Gamma, together with Andromedae, form the large asterism known as the Square of Pegasus." he said.

Impressed, Gemma listened as Abdul told her that Pegasus is from Greek mythology. He explained: "One day Pegasus helped Bellerophon kill the Chimera, a beast that was a combination of a lion, a serpent and a goat. Zeus was greatly angered by this and sent a fly to bite Pegasus and he jumped into the sky."

As they chatted Gemma heard a creaking noise and the painting opened to reveal a doorway and an old man with round, steel-rimmed glasses, clutching a battered brown book.

"Ah! Abdul. *Marhaban*. It's so good to see you. Come in," he said opening the door wider, slightly bowing, and beckoning them in.

"Hello Aalan, *Shokran*," replied Abdul. "This is my friend, Gemma. She's a journalist so careful what you say," he said winking at Aalan, who was shaking hands with Gemma as she looked around, amazed at the huge room with rows upon rows of book shelves and artefacts in glass cases dating back thousands of years.

Her eyes focussed on a helmet in a glass case and she walked over, peering at the object trying to work out who could have worn it and when. It somehow seemed vaguely familiar.

"Ah, you have good taste," said Aalan walking over to join Gemma who was bending down with her head tilted to one side. "Do you know what it is?" he asked.

"It looks Hellenic, Greek," she suggested.

"Yes, yes, but do you know who wore it?" he asked looking at the majestic, ornate, bronze helmet. It had a face plate which opened like a door it - at one time - supported some kind of adornment on top.

"No, I have no idea, but it looks really old," she replied.

"Around circa 450-383. It is a Chalcidian helmet made of bronze and belonged to Alexander the Great, no less, ruler of Macedonia."

"Wow," thought Gemma. "That's someone I'd like to have interviewed. What a fascinating story he would have had to tell." She remembered studying the Greeks during a history lesson at school and how a black stallion called Bucephalus couldn't be ridden by anyone and it was only through Alexander's observation that he realised the horse was afraid of its own shadow, so he turned him towards the sun and got on. A fantastic achievement, for one so young, and clever too! Alexander had made his father, King Phillip, promise the stallion for him if he could ride it!

"This is a special helmet. It is light, bronze, with a pair of cheek pieces, a neck guard looped on each side for the wearer's ears, and a nasal bar to protect the person's nose. In the inner lining a hole was pierced on each cheek piece and a leather lining was inserted," said Aalan.

Fascinated, Gemma asked: "Is this a replica or is it real?"

"Oh, it's real. There are no replicas here. Items are stored here for security. It has been authenticated by a team of experts," he replied, examining the helmet more closely.

"I see," said Gemma. "What happened to Alexander? How did he die?" she asked.

"There are lots of theories like flu, typhoid, malaria, liver failure but no-one knows for sure. I favour one likely theory that he was poisoned by one of his trusted men," said Aalan.

"But why and who would do that? He was a great man who accomplished so much," said Gemma. "Tell me more about the poisoning, Aalan. How was it administered?" she probed further.

Aalan could see she was becoming impatient and walked towards her, both of them staring at the helmet in its square glass enclosure so beautifully and softly illuminated.

"We have no idea, he said. "There had been attempts on Alexander's life before so his food was pre-tasted. The helmet is lined with leather and there are two holes pierced in each cheek piece and perhaps the poison was administered there. It is believed Alexander's trusted royal historian an advisor, Callistenes, poisoned him," explained Aalan.

"But what kind of poison was it?" she asked.

"Well, we don't know for sure," replied Aalan.

"Look, I know this is not normal but would you let me examine the helmet. I have an idea?"

Aalan scratched his bald head. "I don't know. I don't usually do this kind of thing," he replied.

He looked into Gemma's kind eyes and before he knew what he was doing he was opening the glass case. Gemma took out her device, scanned the leather lining, and sent it off to Sparks, her 'tecky' genius, for analysis.

Both Abdul and Aalan watched Gemma curiously. When she noticed them she said: "A gift from a friend from out of town," she explained.

"Thank you, Aalan," she said putting her phone into her fake Armani brown bag and zipping it up. "That is all there is to it," she said.

"Technology is a truly wonderful thing," he replied.

Gemma then walked a few paces, before stopping and looking down at the old weathered object in a glass case. "What's that?" she asked Aalan. The object, obviously a sword about four feet in length had what Gemma thought were runes etched into the blade.

"A Viking sword - but not just any sword, it is the one belonging to Vigor all those centuries ago," said Aalan.

"What's so special about it?" asked Gemma.

"I will tell you what I know. Vigor was a wealthy nobleman who left his homeland of Norway with his men, bound for new trading routes throughout the world. They sailed throughout Europe and perhaps as far as New Zealand. But when they set sail for the Middle East their ships hit a raging storm claiming many long ships.

"After spending a few weeks trekking through the desert trading what they had recovered from their ships, the group came across a Bedouin tribe.

"They were invited into their tent, as was the custom with strangers - even if they were an enemy tradition meant they offered them food and water and protection for three days. After trading and conversing for a day, Vigor noticed one of the tribesmen's swords and asked to see it. After examining it closely he thought it was like no other he had held before.

"The smooth steel metal was perfectly crafted and when one of the Bedouin's plucked a hair from his own head and sliced it in two, Vigor could not fail to be impressed by its superb cutting edge.

"He asked how it was made and one of the Bedouin's ushered him over to the kiln where a sword was being fashioned."

Abdul asked: "Why was that so important to him?"

Aalan replied: "Vigor knew that if his men had these swords they would be invincible against their enemies. A warrior's sword was very precious. To die in battle, sword in hand, meant entry into Valhalla where the warriors would be served endless food and drink by the Valkyries in the afterlife.

"Vigor and his men watched as the Bedouin went through the painstaking process of filtering out impurities in the special white hot furnace, noticing him putting in some white objects, which he later discovered were animal bones. Vigor knew that was the secret ingredient needed to make the steel tougher than any other he had ever seen to create such a powerful sword."

Fascinated by the story Gemma urged Aalan: "What happened next?"

"Vigor knew that when they returned home he would order the blacksmith to create a sword just like the one he had witnessed being forged. He knew it would give him total power and destruction over his enemies.

"Vigor asked if they could trade some silver and wax for the oven. The chief's son, Omar, was in debt but loved his wife dearly and knew that an abundance of silver would impress her, and her friends, who decorated the lining of their veils with coins and silver. The Bedouin women also wore much of their families' jewellery which they then passed on through the generations.

"It was important to her family as sometimes the silver was melted down over and over again in each generation to create new designs for the new wearer.

"The Vikings had a big problem," said Aalan, scratching the side of his lined face.

"What?" asked Gemma and Abdul queried.

"Vigor explained to Omar that they had lost their navigation crystals during the storm at sea and needed them to help return back home to Norway. On cloudy or dark days the Viking explorers when using the sunstone (made from Icelandic Spar) could see the sun within the clouds.

"So in return for the silver, Omar gave him an ornate eloquently-carved wooden box containing sunstone crystals which had been in the tribe for generations.

"The Vikings left the camp and headed for their ships. The blue moon was full when the group reached the shore and loaded up their wares onto the vessels. Vigor set sail in the lead longship. He looked at the sunstone crystals and set them down at the helm as they set sail for home," said Aalan.

Gemma touched the ancient object and was catapulted back in time. It was nightfall when the Norsemen reached the shore and loaded up their wares onto the vessels. She watched as Vigor set sail in the lead long ship and prepared for the journey home.

The thick, white, sea har began to envelop the ships. She heard a voice cry out: "Keep in contact with the others. Don't let us get separated," shouted Vigor to one of his men and ordered another to sound the horn and light torches so the ships knew of each other's approximate location in relation to each other.

The mist and sea had scattered the ships despite their best efforts. Many were never seen again. Fearing for their lives Vigor and his men didn't want to be the latest victims. There was an eerie atmosphere, especially in the dark. The older warriors began telling stories of a sea creature, a giant beast called a Kraken, so powerful it sunk an entire fleet of ships with its massive tentacles. Gemma watched as Vigor bent his head in prayer.

Moments later, Gemma could hear the soft lapping of the oars in the water as the ships made their way through the mist which looked like white clouds engulfing the long vessels. Suddenly, there was a splash - a dolphin jumping, perhaps, thought Gemma. Then a louder and bigger splash and she watched the ship lurch forward and then sideways.

Her eyes followed as the boat bounced through the waves as the warriors rowed harder at their leader's command, the ship cutting through the water with urgency, white sea horses riding high on the crest of the waves, slapping against the sides of the Drakkar.

Gemma held her breath; her palms sweaty, beads of perspiration trickling down the sides of her tanned face as she watched Vigor frantically trying to save his men from going overboard. The ship was sinking and going down fast. Clinging onto the side of the ship for dear life Vigor stretched his arm out over the side, reaching for one of the navigational crystals just before a long red, slimy tentacle shot out and around the mast with the creature tipping the Longship onto its side slowly and determinedly dragging it beneath the water.

Suddenly, Gemma steeled herself as she watched as Vigor grabbed one of the sunstone crystals and thrust it into his shirt pocket as the ship disappeared without a trace - only the large bubbles still visible. He grabbed onto a piece of floating wood that was once a part of this ship and began treading water before looking up at the starry sky.

In the distance Gemma heard what sounded like a horn blow, becoming louder as the minutes passed. She could just make out Vigor looking toward the source and, seeing one of his ships, began waving and they heard him shouting frantically. Then the ship rowed closer before the crew hauled him on board to safety. The cries of men were lost in the darkness and the sea.

Despite being weary from the shipwreck, Vigor was determined to see Hertha as soon as possible. He couldn't wait to see her lovely face which was framed by her waist-long white blond hair. Vigor was besotted with her but questioned if she felt the same way about him. It didn't matter; she would grow to love him once they were married - he was sure - he was an Earl with great lands and riches - she would want for nothing.

Soon after landfall he rode up to the King's palace, Vigor thought about how he was going to arrange for the King's daughter's hand in marriage. He had been away at sea for months and had not heard much news of home.

Dismounting from his horse Vigor strode over to the front door being guarded by four warriors. "I am Vigor; the King is expecting me," he said handing over his sword to one of the guards - remembering to get the blacksmith to forge his new one with the new kiln, brought back from the East. The bones of my ancestors in the making of my sword, shall make me invincible, he smiled, before stepping inside the building.

King Olaf was sitting by the fire being served a bowl of food by a servant. "Ah Vigor, come sit and have some food. The seal and polar bear are excellent," he said.

Vigor sat down and began eating the salted meat and vegetables. "I heard about your ship. You are very lucky to be alive," said the King, wiping his mouth and hands with a piece of cloth. Vigor drank from the wooden cup. He had missed the unique taste of the Mjod beer made from honey, yeast and water.

"Yes, I lost many good men. It is good to be home again after so long," he said putting his drink down on the wooden table.

"So what is it you want to talk to me about, Vigor?" asked the King standing up and walking over to one of the ornate tapestries hanging on the wall.

"I have come to ask for the hand of your daughter, Hertha, Your Majesty," said Vigor. "You know I have much wealth and lands in the North and have brought back riches from the Middle East for you."

The King paused stroking his white beard. "It is true you have done all you have said but it is not possible," he replied.

"Why, my lord? Why?" Vigor asked urgently.

"We need to strengthen our trading with Hibernia (*Ireland*). This is crucial to our success. Hertha has been betrothed to an Earl and has already set sail. I decide what's best. You were away and there was no way of telling you."

Angry and disappointed, Vigor's heart sank. He couldn't believe what King Olaf had just told him. He wanted to strike the King with all his might but knew this would be foolish as he was unarmed and there were too many guards. He would have to think of another plan.

"You may go." said the King, not wanting to dwell any further on the matter.

Vigor bowed before walking over towards the door and out of the palace. *It's not over yet,* he thought, *not by a long shot. She will be mine.*

A month earlier Hertha and her four handmaidens were preparing for the journey to Hibernia. Hertha knew her father's decision to send her there had not been taken lightly. An alliance between the two countries had to be made if her father was to continue to rule.

Hertha left her homeland with a heavy heart not knowing what was in store for her in the foreign land and what her new husband would be like. She thought of Vigor and how they had played and fought together as children. She was fond of him but he was more of a brother to her, though she knew he was in love with her.

Suddenly, she heard shouts from one of the crew on board. Dark ominous-looking rain clouds had formed in the sky and the wind stepped up its pace. Hertha shivered and wrapped her shawl around her shoulders.

"We must take another route if we are to avoid the storm. It would be suicide to attempt it," Dagr, the Captain, explained to Hertha.

"Do what you have to do", she said preparing to be strapped to the ship's mast for safety.

The waves were getting higher and the crew were rowing as hard as they could to escape the impending doom behind them, moving their oars in unison, the fresh salty sea stinging their faces and bodies. There was land ahead.

"Keep rowing! Dagr shouted from the bow of the ship. We can do it. We must."

As the longboat drew nearer to the shore Hertha could see a white beach in front of a dark rocky cliff face. Breathing a sigh of relief, she knew they had escaped the storm but were way off course and had not landed at their original destination.

"Take some men and find some shelter," ordered Hertha. The men left while Hertha and her maidens pondered their fate.

Inger looked up to the top of the cliff. "My lady, look," he said pointing up to the foreboding sharp, ragged rock and to the outline of bodies silhouetted against the pale grey skyline.

"Quick, arm yourselves!" she commanded.

Hertha and her maids –all experienced shield-maidens - prepared for the fight. Their expert training which they received from her father's top warrior would be sorely tested now. Preparing for the voyage Hertha's maidens had woven wool on their looms and made the material into trousers for sailing at sea with a long tunic and long boots made out of goatskin tied with strips of leather.

They wore leather body protectors, shirts of mail and hard leather skull caps to protect their head, their hair tied back with leather tongs. Carrying powerful swords and large round shields, they made their way towards the impending, enemy force surging closer with every movement.

There was no escape, no way out. They were trapped between the stormy sea and their enemy who were now only a few hundred feet away. Hertha steeled herself as the group came closer. She could just make out strange blue markings on their faces and bodies. Who were these people?

Hertha's warriors surrounded their mistress in an instinctive manoeuvre to protect her from what was sure to be an overwhelming onslaught. As the large group approached one man stood out in front and stopped. His tongue was unknown to them but his meaning was clear.

"You are outnumbered. Surrender your weapons," he shouted.

"Never," replied Hertha raising her sword above her head and moving outside the protective circle around her. "We fight to the death," she shouted. Their leader, Calum, was taken aback as he realised it was a woman's voice shouting defiantly back at him.

On closer inspection he could see the feminine outline beneath the outfits and smiled, they were only women, he thought to himself. "Look, put your weapons down," he repeated taking a step forward. "We don't fight women," he said, lowering his sword.

Just then Hertha ran forward and lunged at Calum, his men running forward.

"No!" he shouted, "stay back." His men remained stationary as the two clashed. Calum was staggered by the weight of the blade smashing into his shield and almost lost his balance. What strength for a woman. He would need to be more careful. He noticed how beautiful she was, despite her fierce face which had become encased in a mass of long blond curls which had escaped from its leather binding.

Momentarily distracted, Hertha rained another blow down on the shield which sprang from Calum's hand to the gasps from his men. He would need to do something fast to survive and save face in front of his men. The pair crept around each other like stalking panthers until Calum kicked a handful of sand into Hertha's face, momentarily blinding her, while he leapt on top of her, seizing her sword and throwing it away.

Lying on top of her, his sword at her throat, he breathed over her face. "Give in now?" he asked. Never!" she grimaced but he was too swept away by her beauty to say anything, and jumped up releasing his victim shouting to his men: "Take them to the camp."

One Year Later, West Coast of Scotland

It had been a long time and Vigor was weary. He desperately wanted to go off in search of Hertha but he was forced to fight the King to keep his land.

Now with a new ruler in charge and Vigor's lands secured, he prepared for the voyage to Scotland. His spies had told them that she never arrived in Dublin and had been shipwrecked on the far coast of Caledonia. He was determined to bring her back home where she belonged.

Vigor had packed goods to trade with the Picts - slaves, furs, soapstone, timber, walrus ivory, reindeer antler and hide ropes - anything it would take to get her back. He set sail with his fleet and prayed to Odin for safe passage.

After seven days they arrived at dawn and ran their boats onto the beach for a swift approach. Vigor wanted a peaceful exchange. If it came down to it he would trade his precious navigational crystal for Hertha. However, unbeknown to Vigor, Hertha had fallen in love with Calum MacDonald, the chieftain's son. The couple had a baby daughter, Helga and were living peacefully in the village.

Vigor sent two of his best men ahead telling them that they wanted to trade with the Picts. When the men arrived at the village they threw down their swords as a gesture of peace. Hertha recognised her people who told her why they were here. She listened and discussed it with Calum who agreed that he would see Vigor.

The scouts returned to their fellow men and Vigor and a group of Vikings made their way into the Pictish village. Hertha watched as the group led by Vigor approached. She still recognised his swarthy walk and high head carriage. They had had lots of fun playing and fighting together growing up and it was true she was fond of him but she was not in love with him. Calum was her husband and Helga was a true blessing.

As Vigor approached Hertha and the large group of villagers he was still taken aback by her beauty. "I have come to trade," said Vigor. "Here are furs, reindeer antler, soapstone."

'Soapstone' said Hertha, softly to herself. She had missed it. There were a lot of things that made her homesick but she loved her new life and family.

"What do you want to trade?" asked Calum. "I want my Hertha back home with me," said Vigor.

"Nothing would make me part with her," said Calum.

"Is that your last word?" Vigor asked, drawing his sword.

"My answer is still no!" said Calum anticipating the Viking's response and eyeing up the warrior's powerful sword."

"Then I fight for her." With that Vigor drew his sword lunging at Calum with all his might. A full battle then ensued between the two sides with Hertha running into her home, carefully placing her daughter, Helga, in a wooden cot before picking up her sword and shield and running out to join her husband in the fight which had now moved towards the cliff face.

Distracted at seeing Hertha with sword in hand, Calum shouted to her, and felt the full force of another Viking sword rain down on his round shield knocking him to the ground. Standing over his victim, Vigor raised his sword above his head holding the handle in both hands.

"Prepare to die," he said menacingly before lowering the blade towards Calum's chest. Just at the last moment

Calum rolled away as Vigor plunged the blade into the soil and fell over.

Calum looked over towards a waterfall and could see Hertha surrounded by her maidens desperately trying to fight off the invaders. Suddenly, an arrow struck Hertha's chest sending her over the cliff and onto the dark, craggy rocks below.

Overcome with rage and horror he attacked Vigor and thrust his sword into the Viking's back. As he lay dying, with sword in hand in preparation for Valhalla, he whispered to Calum: "Tell her I love her." In death, he opened his hand to reveal the crystal.

As Calum ran over to where Hertha had fallen. He then climbed down to where Hertha lay on the rocks. One of Hertha's maids had got there first. Fearing the worst he asked urgently "Is she dead?"

"She is still breathing but only just," answered her maid Destin. Her breathing quickened and after a few moments she opened her eyes.

"I thought I'd lost you," he said. Hertha smiled realising she had been given a second chance at life.

Vigor's men took his body and laid it in a boat with his sword, axe, shield, food and drink - all he would need in the afterlife - and sent it out to sea.

Several weeks later Calum and Hertha left with Helga to start a new settlement in Iceland.

Present Day - The Secret Library

"Gemma, Gemma! Are you okay?" said Abdul. "You seemed miles away, as if in some sort of trance," he added with a concerned look on his face.

"I had the weirdest thoughts just then. I was back in the time of the Vikings," she replied, tucking her hair behind her ears and trying to work out what had happened to her.

Aalan walked over towards Abdul and Gemma carrying a small box carved from solid wood with silver and bronze plating. They looked at the intricately carved copper and square circles on the sides and sloping roof and on closer inspection deduced it was designed like a little house or church.

"What is it?" she asked Aalan pointing to the curious-looking object.

"It's a religious reliquary which was carried by the pilgrim monks when the Templar Knights went into battle against the Saracens in this land centuries ago," he replied.

"It seems familiar," said Gemma.

"It was quite a common thing, the design anyway," said Aalan. "Records show there was also a special one made by the monks of Iona, a small island off the west coast of Scotland, and its contents were said to be very revered."

"Long ago the crystal was housed in an abbey on the west coast of Scotland and the monks kept it in the reliquary, called a Brechbannoch. They gave it to King Robert the Bruce on the eve of a great battle at Bannockburn, near Stirling."

Fascinated, Gemma fingered the reliquary, closed her eyes and in a flash was propelled hundreds of years back in time to 1314. She saw a man dressed from head-to-toe in chainmail astride a powerful horse carrying a shield in one hand and a lance, with the reins resting loosely on the animal's neck in the colours of an English knight called De Bohun.

Close by, further up the hill was another man sitting on a small grey pony in front of a group of soldiers. He wore a red lion on a yellow background over his chain-mail and a small gold crown on top of his brown leather helmet. It's the Scots king Robert the Bruce exclaimed Gemma remembering her Scottish history lessons at school.

She watched as the knight on the large war horse -a *destriere* - began galloping with full force at the King, pointing his lance forward. Just as he passed the small pony, the King swerved, raised himself on his mount and with one foot on the ground dodged the incoming lance and clattered his opponent at the back of the helmet with his axe. The blow split both his attackers head and helmet.

As Bruce turned to his men, holding the stump of his axe-shaft, she heard him complain: "I've broken my ane guid axe!" Silhouetted against the early morning light blue sky was Stirling Castle, perched majestically on top of the volcanic rock. Looking over in the distance was a range of familiar-looking green hills, heavily covered with trees.

Nearby, Gemma's eyes were drawn to a small church where she could see the King inside kneeling in prayer. She watched as he walked out of the church, met a group of men dressed in chainmail and spoke to them at length. His voice was confident and he spoke with authority.

As the sun rose, throwing pink and orange hues over the heavy woodland and green fields, King Robert called to his friend and confidante, Bishop Bernard of Arbroath: "Bring before me the Brechbannoch," he commanded, which the bishop duly did. The King opened the lid, took out a small object, placed it in a leather pouch, and then tied it to a hemp rope before carefully lowering it down the grey rough-stone well until it disappeared from sight.

After a few moments he drew the rope back up, untied the pouch, putting the object back in the reliquary and handed it to the Bishop.

After he finished his task King Robert turned to the group of men saying: "Take this water and give it to the troops. I have told you about the Legend of the Pegasus Crystal and its special powers. Tell it to them. The powers of the crystal will make them invincible and victory will be ours."

"Yes Sire," replied the men as they departed to the main body camped in the woods of the hunting Park.

Beads of perspiration began to form along Gemma's hairline and slowly slipped down the sides of her face as the palms of her hands became warm and clammy. Transfixed she watched King Robert, dressed in the distinctive red and yellow Scottish colours of the Lion Rampant, standing within a cluster of his troops.

Another three groups, or *schiltroms,* stepped out in front - the soldiers carrying long spears and resembling the shape of giant hedgehogs. Above the first flew a white and red banner - the flag of the Earl of Carrick, Edward Bruce, Robert's brother. At the front of the second group flew a blue banner with three white stars, under the command of James Douglas and a further group alongside marched under a black banner with wooden vessels, commanded by Angus Og MacDonald and his highlanders.

As they advanced downhill from the trees, a man dressed in long brown robes, carrying a large cross, handed the small brown casket to the king who held it high above his head.

A deathly silence fell over the battlefield as Bruce told his men: "You have drunk water from the well and you know the powers of the Pegasus Crystal. We are unconquerable. We fight for our children our wives and our land. We are bound to stand in battle. This is our day. Seize it men and victory and freedom shall be ours.

"My lords, my people, accustomed to enjoy that full freedom, for which in times gone by the Kings of Scotland have fought many a battle. For eight years or more I have struggled with much labour for my right to the Kingdom and for honourable liberty.

"I have lost brothers, friends and kinsmen. Your own kinsmen have been made captive, and bishops and priests are locked in prison. Our country's nobility has poured forth its blood in war. Those barons you can see before you, clad in mail, are bent upon destroying me and obliterating my kingdom, nay, *our* whole nation.

"They do not believe that we can survive. They glory in their war horses and equipment. For us, the name of the Lord must be our hope of victory in battle. This day is a day of rejoicing to celebrate the birth of John the Baptist. With Our Lord Jesus as commander, Saint Andrew and the martyr Saint Thomas shall fight today with the saints of Scotland for the honour of their country and their nation.

"If you heartily repent for your sins you will be victorious, under God's command. As for offences committed against the Crown, I proclaim a pardon, by virtue of my royal power, to all those who fight manfully for the kingdom of our fathers."

As the sun shone brightly against the blue sky, a huge roar rippled through the heaving mass of Scotsmen as King Robert gave the order to advance and Gemma watched as the three massive groups of soldiers carrying long spears continued marching downhill. The fourth *schiltrom,* commanded by the King followed behind.

Once out in the open in full view of the enemy the entire Scots army dropped to their knees and said The Paternoster - The Lord's Prayer in Latin - asking for forgiveness for their sins.

It was an amazingly emotional moment and Gemma felt tears welling up in her eyes as she saw the warriors, who were clearly outnumbered, courageously take on the enemy who had roused themselves and were advancing on their war horses. As they closed together the cries of men and whinnies from horses dying and the putrid stench of blood and gore made her feel sick as each side rained terrible blows on each other.

She felt a hand on her arm. "Gemma, Are you alright?" said a voice. Gemma jolted and opened her eyes trying to forget the horrific scene and carnage which had unfolded before her.

"I'm okay, I think. I could see what happened at the battle. It felt like I was actually there," she said, the colour draining from her face.

Aalan asked her: "What clan do you belong to Gemma?" "I'm a MacDonald," she replied, taking a sip of water from a clear crystal glass he had handed her.

"Ah, your ancestor Angus Og MacDonald fought at the King's side, the MacDonald's, Lords of the Isles." he said.

"You seem to know a lot about history." said Abdul.

"Yes, knowledge is my life and I am dedicated to it." Aalan replied.

"Bruce won the day and Edward the Second was escorted from the field by his knights and fled to Dunbar on the East Coast before taking ship for Berwick. The Scots captured many English knights and held them for ransom but he also returned the bodies of slain ones to their families. It was a remarkable victory which won the independence of Scotland and his humility in victory earned him many admirers and great respect." said Aalan.

"What ransom did the King ask for in return for the knights?" asked Abdul.

"Years ago Edward stole the Stone of Destiny from Scone Abbey near Perth and took it to Westminster. Scotland's Kings were crowned on the stone, except for Bruce, so this would have been a good bargaining tool for Bruce to trade." replied Aalan.

"However, it is whispered that Edward did not take the real stone. Fearing it was going to be stolen, abbey monks at Scone Palace hid the real stone in the River Tay or Dunsinane Hill and replaced it with a replica. It has even been rumoured that Macbeth buried the stone at the bottom of his castle on the hill of Dunsinane. If this is true that could be why Bruce did not request its return."

"Is the well from which the men drank the special water from still there?" asked Gemma,

"Yes it's near the church in Cambusbarron. It is called 'Bruce's Well' and it is thought to have healing properties to anyone who drinks from it ever since that time. It was also known as 'Christ's Well' in earlier times," said Aalan.

"Aalan, what happened to the crystal after the Battle of Bannockburn?" asked Gemma trying to piece the bits of the jigsaw puzzle together.

"King Robert entrusted the Monymusk Reliquary as it was known, containing the Pegasus Crystal to the monks in Cambuskenneth Abbey, for safe keeping. The Abbey was also the setting for the first Scottish Parliament.

"It was hidden there for many years until the time of the Scottish Reformation when there was looting and burning so the monks, fearing for their safety and that of their precious crystal, supposedly hid it in a small hermitage located in the woods nearby. Before the Battle of Sheriffmuir in 1715, as tradition had it, from centuries ago the Clan MacDonald had always had a crystal before going into battle.

"Alan MacDonald, Clan MacDonald of Clanranald, was tasked with delivering the crystal on the eve of battle. However, they arrived late and during a melee' the crystal was lost.

"Alan and his men set off over the hills to Sheriffmuir to join the Earl of Marr and fight the Duke of Argyll, who led the Government's army but on the way to the battlefield the MacDonalds encountered a scouting party for the Duke and in the skirmish they were defeated.

"The MacDonalds and Earl of Marr went into the battle without the crystal. Alan was severely wounded and died the next day. Whilst neither side admitted defeat the Earl's withdrawal signalled the end of the first Jacobite uprising."

"Jacobite," said Gemma. "It was strange to hear you say it."

"I hope I pronounced it correctly," said Aalan.

"Yes," replied Gemma. It was from the latin *Jacobis,* meaning 'follower of King James'.

"But come over here, we don't have much time," said Aalan pointing over to an old brown table. "Sit down, please," he beckoned. Gemma and Abdul sat down in the tall-backed chairs and watched as the old man sat down and clasped his withered hands.

"My people are descendants of an ancient civilisation who worshipped in a cave thousands of years ago. The cave contained many crystals; crystals which they used for healing. Life was simple but good and peaceful until the mother crystal went missing.

"We don't know what happened to it but it has a special power and significance to the cave. It has been lost for centuries and we had all but given up hope of finding it again," he said looking over at Abdul.

"So, have you found it?" asked Gemma desperate to know more about this mysterious crystal. Abdul looked into Gemma's green eyes which had darkened and were flashing with excitement.

"You have the crystal, Gemma."

She stared at Aalan with a puzzled look.

"I don't have a crystal," she replied.

"But you do," insisted Aalan. "You've had it all along and it's been guiding you here all this time."

"I don't understand," said Gemma.

"This is your destiny, Gemma," said Aalan. "It is written in the Legend of the Pegasus Crystal, a fair-haired girl who was born with a sacred veil over her face from an ancient tribe from the North will return the crystal to its home. Through the centuries the crystal appears to people in times of need but its powers are fading and it needs to be returned to regenerate with the other crystals in the cave to restore its power," he said.

"When we were in my father's jet you told me about being born with a 'hallihoo' over your head and I recognised the significance. Too much to be chance," said Abdul.

Gemma put her hand up to her neck, but the pouch was gone. Of course, she had forgotten to put it back on after showering that morning and had asked Sharon to bring it to the hotel.

"Yes, But I don't have it on me," she insisted. Aalan rose up from the old wooden table and Gemma noticed the ring on his finger was in the shape of Pegasus.

"You have been wearing the crystal for so long it is now part of you. It has changed who you are and your very essence," he said softly. Just as he was about to explain further his mobile phone trilled into life. "Yes, yes, I understand."

Turning to Gemma and Abdul he said, "You have to leave right away. Strangers are here and asking questions about you. They will stop at nothing to get the crystal. You must return the crystal to the cave before it's too late for us all.

"There's only one way to escape. Fortunately, we plan for contingencies," he said walking towards a door and then opening a cupboard alongside, he lifted out what looked like two backpacks. "Here take these and go up to the top of the building," he said, thrusting two packs at Abdul.

"No, we can't. I don't have my stone; I mean the crystal," protested Gemma.

"You must hurry, there is not much time left. You must go now. You cannot leave the way you came in," said Aalan.

The pair ran out of the room and through another door to the stairwell, where they headed up and a few minutes later came out onto the massive roof of the hotel, big enough to play a tennis match on.

Gemma saw the helipad, sensing an unwanted flying experience.

"Put this on!" said Abdul pushing a package into Gemma's arms.

"Wait, I'm not going up in that thing and definitely not in this dress!" she protested.

"Look there is no other way," shouted Abdul taking his knife out of his pocket before ripping Gemma's long dress to just below her knees. "No excuse now, Gemma. We're not going up but down! Come on, let's go. This is our only chance of survival," insisted Abdul, who then quickly helped strap the parachute onto Gemma.

Reluctantly, Gemma put it on while Abdul took her hand.

"We're going to run and jump and it's going to be okay. I've done this before," he said. Gemma threw him a look. "You need to trust me," he said.

Just then the door they had came through burst open and three men drew weapons and took aim. Gemma acted quickly. "Robson, Midnight. Activate 5d now!" She commanded. Gemma speedily tapped on her and Abdul's image on the device strapped to her leg and the device immediately duplicated their five dimensional replicas, about five metres away. The sound of gunfire split the air. The gunmen confused by the dual images had selected the wrong targets.

Taking advantage of the confusion, Abdul grabbed Gemma's hand and together they raced for the edge of the platform and over it, into space. Bang, bang ... more shots fired. Looking into his deep brown eyes, Gemma knew she could trust him and down they went still holding hands. After a moment later Gemma heard Abdul's voice: "Gemma! Gemma! Pull the chord. Pull it!"

Gemma glanced to her right shoulder and saw the red rip-chord trailing behind her. Her heart was beating fast.

"I can't, I can't reach!" she yelled before Abdul quickly leaned over, pulled the chord immediately she was yanked upwards and her world began to spin. When she countered the spin using the rigging lines she then began floating downwards like a bird towards the blue sea. She looked around but could not see any sign of Abdul.

Her world continued to spin then stabilize and she noticed the wind was taking her offshore.

The orange and yellow sun was getting low on the horizon, almost gently caressing the skyline as Gemma tried to get her bearings, looking around, relieved the water was coming up fast. There was the creek and she could just make out the *Abras* (water taxis) and boats, which had appeared so small before, becoming bigger as the sea was getting nearer. Gemma remembered Duncan's words of advice when he was teaching her about parachuting into water. 'What you don't want,' he advised, was the device that saved your life coming down on top of you in the water and getting entangled in it and drowning.

'The idea or practice is to turn and undo the quick-release device and sit in the bottom part of the harness. Pull down on the rigging lines (or use the air-brake lines if you have them) and release when about ten feet from the surface. Slip out of the harness. The sudden lack of weight should allow the parachute to lift up and travel on before landing. Hopefully, not down on top of you.'

Splash! Gemma plunged into the blue water legs together. She began swimming frantically towards the surface. Breaking through, instinctively, she turned to assess her direction in relation to the shore. She looked around for Abdul but couldn't see any sign of him. Her heart sank when she looked at the shoreline. It looked a long way off and even though Gemma was a strong swimmer she knew it was going to be tough to make it. However, the adrenaline of her abrupt descent was still running high and she began to swim to shore.

She ploughed through the waves using the breast stroke, which was a good stroke to pace yourself and allow you a good field of vision ahead. Lifted by the natural buoyancy of the salt water, Gemma swam until she felt the build up of lactic acid in her tired muscles.

Still, she reasoned, she was making good time and decided to tread water for a while to catch her breath.

She could hear seabirds in the distance and the water was darkening a little with the receding sun. While the cramps eased Gemma floated on her back, and closed her eyes, remembering the feeling of weariness when walking in the mountains of Scotland when she felt her lungs would burst if she took another step towards the top of the Munro in Glencoe, which meant the 'Glen of Weeping' after the Glencoe well-documented massacre. While it was a magical place, Gemma always felt shivers down her spine every time she went there and a tinge of sadness. Were her ancestors trying to telling her something?

Gemma recalled walking in the 'Lost Valley' (*Coire Gabhail*) where her ancestors, the MacDonalds, hid their rustled cattle from the rival clans centuries ago.

But now the only thing she could feel right now was her body becoming heavier, the sea inviting her to stay forever. She righted herself and it was then, about twenty feet away, between her and the shore, Gemma saw the shadow under the water. It circled her warily, sliding in and out of her view with intimidating ease. Gemma followed its action as best she could.

She recalled Duncan's words of advice. 'Sharks are natural predators. They attack from below and behind with sudden swiftness. If you find yourself stalked by one, keep it in sight.

"Like all predators, they don't want to get hurt, as they cannot feed themselves and might die. So they look for the easy option such as the sick, the old (or young) or the unwary. No unnecessary splashing. It might excite the shark further, or attract others nearby. Try and read its body language.'

Gemma watched as the dark grey shape moved towards her, getting a little closer and then moving out a little again. Doesn't seem overly aggressive, she hoped. She reasoned that the creature may have been with her since she entered the water and her hasty splash into the sea may have attracted it. That would also be its best chance of a surprise attack, thought Gemma.

'Do I wait it out and hope it loses interest and leaves? Or do I continue toward shore?' She tried to balance her thoughts. It was then she saw the second movement out of the corner of her eye. That made her mind up. Gemma went back to her breast stroke and tried to make no surface splashing mistakes.

When she was about four hundred yards from shore, the shadow turned in front of her blocking her route to shore. It then turned toward Gemma, swiftly closing the distance turning to her right side at the last moment.

Gemma, her heart in her mouth, turned to follow its direction. The creature surfaced barely two feet from her startled face. "EEEEEEEK, EEEEEEK!" it cried.

Yikes! An astonished Gemma realised, it was a dolphin! The dolphin blew water from its air-hole on its head, stopped and gazed into Gemma's eyes. The eyes she looked into were hypnotic. It flipped its left fin at her playfully and seemed to want to ... invite her? Gemma reached out to touch the magnificent creature in front of its back fin.

The dolphin moved forward slowly, until it realised Gemma had good purchase in front of the fin and then it began to tow her slowly to shore. As it did so, it picked up the pace gradually, as it sensed Gemma's confidence grow. The shoreline came up quickly and as she was towed along Gemma could see two or three other shapes escorting them in. She had read of dolphins rescuing people in difficulties at sea and now she knew it was true. She realised she was in good company.

They were surrounding her and she was overwhelmed by being welcomed into their family. On reaching shore Gemma turned to thank her saviour. Her left hand under its smooth, slippery, chest and the right hand on its head she peered into the eyes of this fantastic creature with gratitude and she nodded. She felt a connection; a different species, a different mammal, so far apart, but with a common bond of friendship. What was it she saw in the creature's eyes? There was friendship or compassion, that's for sure. Gemma realised she was seeing in its eyes all the things in all the seas it had swam through. And yet, there was a deep sadness too. Intelligence! That's what she realised she was seeing. Gemma wondered how she could really thank her saviour.

The smiling dolphin seemed to understand; I can save you but you cannot save me. With this the dolphin slipped from Gemma's hands and headed off to join its companions. Gemma walked a few steps up the sand and sat down facing out to sea. Exhausted both mentally and physically she could feel the ripples of water dripping down from her tired body onto the glittering golden ground. Not quite how she thought the evening would go.

Abdul, she remembered. *I wonder where he is at this moment in time? I hope he's OK,* she thought softly to herself, tears welling up in her eyes as she gazed up at the sky. After a while she sat up, crossed her legs, hugged her knees to her chest, and looked over at the tall glistening structure built in the shape of a sail.

Suddenly, she felt a hand across her mouth rough fingers pulling her hands behind her back and feeling them being tied with a coarse rope.

"Don't struggle and you won't get hurt," said a gruff male voice in a thick Arab accent, picking her up, bundling her into the backseat of a black car and lay on her on her side. She felt a sharp pain in her leg and suddenly she felt very, very tired. The engine roared and the vehicle sped off into the distance. Gemma's heart was beating as fast as a rabbit. She feared for her life until darkness overtook her.

Finally, after what seemed like an eternity and was certainly hours, the vehicle stopped. The door opened and Gemma was dragged out and carried into a black tent and thrown down in a corner.

Gemma lay on a stripped rug. In the corner, when her eyes adjusted, she could see the outline of a shadowy figure sitting on cushions smoking from a *Hokkah.* The sweet aromatic smell from the tobacco infusion filled Gemma's nostrils, sparking off a rumbling sound in her stomach with the realisation that she was very hungry.

“Where am I? Who are you?” Gemma asked straining her eyes to get a closer look at her kidnapper. At first she thought it was Abdul.

"You are wondering why you are here? I will tell you. You have something of interest and all you have to do is tell me where it is," he said still hidden from Gemma's sight.

"What would that be exactly?" said Gemma, rubbing sleep from her eyes focussing on the mysterious figure.

"Why, the *crystal* of course. We know you do not have it on you. Where is it?" his voice becoming more urgent.

After a few moments 'silence she heard the man get up, walk over to her. A look of horror appeared on her face. It was Khalid, Abdul's twin brother, carrying a curved dagger with a jewelled handle. Gemma's heart skipped a beat. He stood behind her, bent down and cut the rope binding her hands.

He said: "My brother seems enamoured with you but believe me when I say that I am not. You stand before me and my rightful place as head of this Kingdom. No one will come between me and my destiny, not my brother or you."

Gemma felt her resolve rise and said: "You are not your brother by a long way and Abdul wouldn't need a crystal to feel good about himself." Khalid sighed, as if he were talking to a child.

"Escape is futile. My men will return with some refreshments and we will talk later. Please consider this carefully," he said, before walking out of the tent.

Gemma shivered at the thought of him coming back. Over in the corner she spotted her silver clutch bag. The last time she had seen it was when she put the chain diagonally over her shoulder before base jumping from the top of the hotel.

She walked over in her bare feet, her fuschia pink toenails broken and chipped before picking up the bag, opening it to discover her lipstick and hairbrush but no mobile.

Holding the hairbrush and hoping it would work after being in the ocean, she pressed the design on the back, activating the tracking device. When the light came on it indicated success. Thank goodness for Sparkie and his inventions, she smiled to herself.

A few minutes later a guard appeared with some Mezes and tea, beckoning Gemma to eat. She shook her head but the guard drew his handgun and Gemma realised it would be wise to do what he said. She ate the food hungrily, washing it down with the sweet tea. It felt so good. After she finished the meal the guard bound her hands in front of her and left the tent.

How am I going to get out of this? I'm helpless and my arms are bound. Lying on the cold ground she thought back to the Maeatae and Eithne on Dumyat, stuck in a freezing bog for days with little to eat, hiding from her enemy, enduring hardship and danger and finding the courage to face death ... and King Robert the Bruce and his army, heavily outnumbered but prepared to fight and die for their country no matter the odds, never giving up no matter how big the challenge.

I've got to do something, Gemma thought to herself before wriggling over to her clutch bag and opening it she took out her hairbrush. Pressing the tracker activator on the rear she then worked her hands over the brush till she felt the small catch and turned it, revealing the spike with the serrated edge. She managed to cut the tight ropes from around her wrists and then pretended to tie them again so the guard would not be suspicious.

I will have to wait and pick the right moment ... one false move and Gemma knew the consequences.

Chapter Six

Qamar State -The Rescue

Prince Abdul stood in the darkness of the desert night 80 miles from the nearest village, contemplating what was ahead. Turning to his friend Anees, he said: "It is now time to act. Let's pray that God smiles on us and we will meet again in this life."

"*Inchallah,*" replied Anees, nodding.

It was time to act. Contingencies had been made and now all that was left was the execution.

Prince Abdul moved swiftly along the side of the dunes that formed a valley more than a mile long and he stayed about four feet below the crest. Crouching down, he took short, fast steps against the shifting sands moving like a panther, smooth and purposeful, remembering how his father had taught himself and Khalid the ways of the desert as young children. He moved assuredly and quietly like a wild animal, his focus and resolve absolute. Abdul was incensed that something like this could happen to a guest in his country, let alone someone he cared for. They had known each other only a few entrancing months but in that time a bond of friendship had formed. Now because of this her life was in danger. He blamed himself and cursed the perpetrators.

Further down to the base of the valley he soon spotted the desert encampment. Half a dozen palm trees formed the vegetation of the old oasis, popular with traders heading for the coast, and nearby the four tents, two black off-road vehicles, both of which he thought he recognised.

Even in the darkness Abdul could make out the shapes. Only one of the tents was guarded, two figures stood either side of the entrance so he knew that that was the one which held Gemma. He steeled himself for action and cursed the evil that exists in mankind, for kidnapping Gemma.

After their abrupt descent from the roof of the Burj-Al-Arab Hotel, Abdul had landed in the sea further east than Gemma and managed to get a ride on a water taxi to safety.

It was only after a frantic call to Gemma's private detective friend Sharon that Abdul found out that it was Aquil's men who had snatched Gemma. Sharon had been in the hotel looking for the pair when their abrupt descent had caught the attention of everyone. By the time Sharon had got to the shore she had witnessed Gemma being taken forcibly. Her professionalism had kicked in and she noted the vehicle registration plate and a description of the three men who took Gemma.

Sharon told Abdul: "I ran the plates - Qamar plates - and found the vehicle that took Gemma was unregistered. You know what that means?"

Abdul nodded.

State owned or stolen, I'll find out which, she thought to herself.

"But, why Gemma?" Abdul asked Sharon.

"Time will solve that mystery," said Sharon. "We need to figure out where she is and fast before it's too late." Sharon called a few contacts in the police and the Chronicle to see if they had heard or could find out anything.

A few minutes later a light flickered on Abdul's tablet. He opened it up, pressed the touchpad a few times and paused. "I know where she is," he said excitedly.

"Well stop dawdling and get after her," replied Sharon impatiently forgetting that he was a Prince.

Gemma was being held at a secret desert location approximately 80 miles south of Jaball. Abdul called trusted friends and made arrangements for her rescue, then promising to keep Sharon informed of his progress, raced back to Jaball City. Once Abdul had reached Jaball, he changed clothes and headed to Jaball local airport, civilian section, to prep his aircraft. His earlier call to Anees had instructed his friend to proceed to a valley near the camp, where he believed Gemma was being held, as quickly as he could and await his arrival. Anees had brought the extra fuel and supplies Abdul had requested and waited impatiently at the rendezvous.

Late in the evening Abdul arrived by microlight aircraft. Nearly seven hours had passed and he was concerned about what might have happened to Gemma in that time. He was also starkly aware that the light comes early to the desert and he reckoned he had two hours at most to get to Gemma and make their escape.

Anees stood up when he heard the buzzing of the engine and soon saw the aircraft curving in to land in the valley as arranged. As soon as Abdul was safely down he turned the aircraft around and Anees set about topping up the fuel tank, as he had done so many times before.

Staying hidden beneath the dunes until he was past the camp, Abdul approached one of the tents at a right-angle. He stealthily flitted between the trees like a shadow, gliding over the sand as silent as a cat stalking its prey.

Going down the side of the nearest tent and round behind it, he then silently passed the tent with the guards on the other side, moving towards the vehicles. Pausing for a moment to listen, he drew his curved dagger from beneath his black, traditional Arab robes before piercing the rear tyres and spares on both vehicles and one of the front tyres on the nearest vehicle.

Returning to the second tent, he raised his dagger, pushing it through the matted fabric, slowly bringing it down parallel to the corner pole. When he had finished it would hang in such a way it would not be noticed unless touched. The dagger was so sharp the material fell away with little resistance.

Peering through the gap he saw an oil lamp hanging from the centre cross-pole and closed his right eye so that he would not lose all of his night vision. There, bundled lying on the floor in a foetal position was Gemma, with her hands behind her back.

The sound of ripping material alerted Gemma. As she prepared to separate the loose chord from around her wrists she felt a hand on her calf.

She gasped audibly as she saw the gleaming, serrated blade and the dimly-lit face behind it.

"No, no," she implored.

"It is Abdul," he whispered softly. As he began to remove the gag on her mouth he stopped.

Gemma looked to her left, over his right shoulder.

One of the guards had entered the tent. "I'm sorry my Prince, I did not know?" he uttered, thinking it was Khalid as they were both identical, then stopped as he saw the dagger. The guard's eyes widened with astonishment but before he could raise the alarm Abdul lunged and kicked the man hard in the stomach and he crumpled forward onto the mat.

In a flash Abdul was on him and the dagger dug deep into the guard's brain targeting the cerebellum. Seconds later another guard appeared holding a Russian-made semi-automatic weapon.

The second guard assessed the situation and tried to bring his machine pistol to bear on Abdul but before he could do so, there was a loud clang and the hanging lamp, swung by Gemma, hit the guard squarely in the face causing him to fall backwards towards the door unconscious.

"Lights out!" said Gemma. "I knew my hairbrush would come in handy. Sparks' idea of fitting it with a tracking device was sheer genius," she said.

"Where did you learn that?" inquired Abdul, softly.

"Finishing School," Gemma replied.

"Come we must hurry," Abdul said softly grabbing Gemma by the arm and leading her out the rear of the tent before they both crouched down. Abdul picked up a puzzled Gemma.

"What are you doing?" she asked.

"I'll explain later," he replied, carrying her to the other side of the dune and set her down. "Time is now at a premium, said Abdul softly. What are you wearing on your feet?"

"Sandals," replied Gemma equally softly.

"Remove them! Abdul advised, and put them down the back of your belt. When we get clear of the camp we will have to move quickly, bare feet are better in soft sand. We have about a mile to go."

He turned round and curious, Gemma did the same. They then reversed out the way Abdul had entered the camp for about fifty yards. Retracing his steps might not completely fool their pursuers but it might buy them some time. They then turned around and after a glance that indicated a change of pace, he led her away.

After they had travelled quickly approximately five hundred yards, they were both panting. Their exertions began to be heavy going, running in the deep, cold-beige-coloured sand. Lactic acid formed in Gemma's calves and slim thighs and they began to burn. Abdul heard her panting and stopped, crouching down and she copied him. They were on the same wave-length.

Listening to ascertain if they had been discovered, Abdul said: "We're about half-way there. Can you keep going?" She nodded and after about ten seconds they moved off again, re-doubling their efforts. Gemma was beginning to believe they would make it, too, when they heard a commotion in the distance behind them and the revving up of vehicles, the sound carrying far in the desert at night.

At the top of the valley the ground opened up into three other potential escape routes. Crossing the valley floor they took the left hand fork and ahead Gemma could make out a shape in the darkness.

As they got closer, her heart sank when she realised what it was. He had only brought that infernal microlight with him. It was a joke between them since they had first met. On the ground in the stygian darkness the microlight looked like an odd-shaped prehistoric bird or an ungainly, giant bat.

Gemma knew flying as a necessary evil, but Abdul loved it. He had been bitten by the flying bug as a young boy when he was introduced to falconry. On his twenty-first birthday his father had granted both brothers a special wish. For Abdul the answer was simple. He went to Australia for flying lessons and this, in turn, made him buy the XT912 microlight and he flew as often as he could. Nothing else allowed him the freedom to travel and see the land he loved like no other.

As they reached the red-bodied machine, he took off his robes and head dress and beckoned Gemma to replace her footwear. He also handed her a crash helmet equipped with a microphone and a brown, leather, bomber-style jacket.

As he put on his own helmet he told her: "When I start up the noise will let everyone know where we are. We must take off as quickly as we can and lose ourselves in the dunes until we are clear."

Gemma nodded, putting on the jacket and climbing on the rear seat of the XT-912 Streak, Australian-made flying machine.

She strapped herself in the rear seat above the fuel tank and plugged in her headset/microphone. Abdul prepped the machine for take-off and drained off a little fuel. The last thing they wanted on take-off was the engine to falter as the feed was interrupted by condensation in the fuel lines caused by the bitterly cold desert night.

Satisfied, Abdul climbed into the front seat of the tandem aircraft, fastened his straps and automatically went through the start-up procedure. Though the desert night was bitterly cold, it was still way above the minimum operating temperature needles for the XT-912. As Abdul switched on the battery their headsets crackled and the electric back-lit control dials danced into life.

Abdul turned to Gemma and her headset hissed: "Once I start up we have to wait until the engine warms up before take-off. They will know exactly where we are," he said. Gemma nodded feeling the icy air bite into her bones despite the warm leather jacket.

At the camp their escape had been discovered. Prince Khalid was infuriated demanding to know how it happened. He did not suffer fools lightly. Calling on all of his men he seethed: "How did this happen?"

Khalid knew it was Abdul as he recognised his methods which had been taught to them both by his father. Before the man could answer Khalid yelled: "Never mind, get after them!"

"Akim, take one group and follow the tracks you find to their source." He remembered the days of his childhood and the games he played with his brother, walking backwards to disguise his direction was not an unknown trick to him. "Have Rashid take the others and track back to where he entered camp," yelled Khalid.

"Yes, Your Highness, said Akim, bristling with indignation. I do not know how to apologize for the incompetence of these dogs!"

"Then don't. There will be time for that later," countered Khalid.

One of the men returned to report. "Master, the tracks lead beyond the dune and head north following the line of the hills. The tracks show three people entering the camp but as yet none have been found leaving!" He added: "The vehicles have been disabled too ..."

Khalid recognized his brother's handiwork. "They cannot have gone far, go quickly, follow the tracks to their source," he commanded and Rashid led the men running towards the hills. In the distance, a high-pitched buzzing sound pierced the night air, a beacon of discovery. Khalid remembered the days of their childhood and the games he played with his brother.

As the XT-912 crabbed its way forward on its tricycle undercarriage, Abdul worked the foot pedals one way then the other searching for the first of the white rocks acting as runway markers Anees and he had marked and aligned earlier.

The Rotax Bombardier 80hp engine whined at 200 revolutions-per-minute as it sought to reach the minimum oil temperature of 50 degrees before they could take off the ground. Then he saw it. Turning left round the white rock he pointed the microlight on a compass bearing he took earlier that day and applied the parking brake.

As they pointed ahead into the darkness, Abdul gently increased the revolutions using the foot throttle only. He set the trim to 'fast' and watched the oil temperature gauge.

"Nearly there," he said to Gemma. "Not before time. Look we've got company," she replied looking over at the dark shapes crossing the sides of the valley and advancing quickly toward them.

That'll have to do, Abdul thought, and released the parking brake. The microlight slowly gathered speed initially, despite the sand on the valley floor being quite firm. Increasing the foot throttle to the full, 5,000 revs and using his feet to keep on course, the aircraft seemed reluctant to leave the ground. Suddenly, the sound of automatic gunfire rang out. Abdul looked up at the wing overhead and was startled to see it gleaming with condensation. He knew from experience that this would increase the take-off distance considerably and in the air, would affect the performance of the machine.

After what seemed like an eternity, the microlight eased off the ground and climbed steadily. The surrounding dunes masked the sound of the engine and distorted its location. In the blackness of the desert night, the beige wing overhead - which gave such good camouflage on the ground - could be their undoing in the sky.

A few hundred feet off the ground and Abdul eased off the climb and prepared to make a slow turn to the left when suddenly there were loud noises, CRACK, CRACK CLANG! Bullets tore through the microlight but Abdul continued his turn and the harsh barking of the Russian automatic weapons soon fell behind.

Changing course and direction every thirty seconds they soon lost their attackers. In the darkness behind they could see red and green tracer rounds lighting up the sky with frustration more than accuracy. Safely out of range Abdul set course north for the coast. He climbed slowly to 600 feet and eased out of the turn, reducing his speed to a cruising preference of 55-60 knots.

Turning back to Gemma, he asked "Are you ok?" Gemma nodded enthusiastically, the engine seriously disrupting any attempt at speaking, even with the microphone.

He smiled. "We are about thirty minutes to the coast give or take a few and then we'll turn right and follow the coastline east over Jaball City and then back to the stables."

Despite the heavy jacket, Gemma felt a shiver travel down her spine. The wind rummaged at her clothes like thousands of tiny hands and as she gazed around at the featureless desert; she felt drained after the initial adrenaline rush high. Being shot at will do that to you. As she gazed at the featureless desert, she felt chilled.

As they flew on, the dark veil of night turned navy blue, stars faded and disappeared and yet the transformation continued. Gemma closed her eyes for some short periods and then heard Abdul's voice. "Look over there, the coast."

The sky changed into a light grey colour and over on the horizon to their left the first orange beams radiated the sky. Gemma looked straight ahead and could just make out a line of waves crashing towards the shore.

A little while later Abdul turned the aircraft to the right. The XT-912 microlight was a type steered by 'weight-shifting', that is to say the pilot steered by means of a bar in front of him which he pushed left to go right and vice-versa. As he looked up he was astounded to see two ragged holes in the wing overhead and about three feet to his right. The B' Streak wing was made of 6oz Dacron and was immensely strong. However, he would have to be careful not to overstress the structure.

As they flew on up the coast following the main city road, the sun peeked over the horizon behind them and lit up the way.

Abdul glanced down to his left. "Look, we have an escort," he said. Gemma turned her head in the direction he was pointing. At first she couldn't believe what she was seeing.

Birds, she couldn't make them out yet, were heading in the same direction, to the rich feeding grounds of the City estuary. Abdul reduced speed and expertly tried to avoid the flock of flamingos but it was too late, in a flash they were engulfed in flurries of pink and white feathers, as the birds surrounded them for a short while in formation.

Fortunately, the birds fell behind and below as the microlight easily out-distanced them. But not before both had several eyeball-to-eyeball encounters. The birds, having inspected this strange flying craft and its occupants, seemed satisfied and went their separate ways. Gemma breathed a sigh of relief.

"Not far to go now. I'm going to set down near my father's stables at the racecourse. If we go to the airport we might get a hot reception," said Abdul.

"Fine by me," replied Gemma. "I just want to get back down on terra firma in one piece."

Crossing over the outskirts of Jaball City, Abdul turned south again for the racecourse which he could see in the distance.

"There it is. We'll start our descent soon. Tighten your restraints," he advised.

Gemma noticed Abdul seemed preoccupied and he adjusted their course slightly. Her stomach leapt as they rose and fell as if borne by a large wave. "Is everything alright?" She asked.

"She's handling differently than usual," he replied. "I can't get her to turn quite right. The difference is marginal and all the instruments are reading correctly. Not far now ... we'll start our descent."

No sooner had the words left his lips when they heard a loud CRACK! Then the microlight dropped suddenly and uncontrollably, as one of the supporting struts of the right wing snapped.

Tumbling over and over like some grief-stricken prehistoric bird they were tossed around and around accompanied by the scream of the engine. Parts of the wing tore off and were shredded by the propeller blades, pieces of which were thrown back at Abdul and Gemma who felt the bits smacking off her helmet.

She grasped the sides of her chair like a motorcycle pillion passenger to counteract the g-forces. As the aircraft rapidly plunged downwards with astonishing rapidity, suddenly she was aware that she could no longer hear the engine.

Gemma closed her eyes screaming: "Abdul, help!" the colour draining from her tanned face.

Abdul had immediately started to carry out the emergency procedures by cutting the power to the engine and stopping the fuel. To do this under a controlled environment was demanding but under emergency conditions it was practically overwhelming. He activated the BRS-5 and, with a shuddering jolt, they were jerked upwards momentarily as the ballistic parachute deployed. Then they headed back down again in a worryingly fast descent.

As Gemma struggled to comprehend what was happening there was a sickening thud as the remains of the aircraft, with them both still attached, smacked off the corrugated roof of a building, rolled, and then fell a further 20 feet to the ground.

The remains of the aircraft lay broken and shattered around them. Lying flat on her back Gemma opened her eyes but could not see. Her nose filled with the acrid smell of aviation fuel.

As she lay motionless on the hard ground in the darkness she could hear the faint sound of a horse whinnying in the distance.

Chapter Seven

Jaball Hospital – Post Crash

It was the sterile antiseptic smell that hit her nostrils like a freight train, reminding Gemma of being in hospital as a young child when she had had her tonsils removed. The painful memories of the fear and anguish she felt after her parents left her in the children's ward in Edinburgh came flooding back.

They had brought a pink and white plastic tea set with dark grey flowers on it for her to play with while she was recovering from the operation and Gemma was so excited with her new toy. After a while playing with it visiting time was up and she cried as her parents walked out of the ward without her. Even to this day the thought of hospital jelly and ice cream made her want to throw up.

Slowly, very slowly she opened her emerald-green eyes and realised she was lying on her back staring up at a cold, clinical white ceiling with a spotlight staring down right above her head. Her perfect white blonde hair was now matted and coarse.

She looked up and then moved her eyes to the left and to the right trying to work out where she was and what she was doing lying on her back.

Got to find out what's going on, she rationalized but just as she was about to get up she heard a female voice nearby talking in Arabic. Gemma seemed completely immobile.

"What am I doing here? What's going on? I have to get out of here. I have to get back to the office," said a flustered Gemma, her cheeks getting redder and warmer by the second despite the heavily air conditioned room.

A nurse glided effortlessly and almost noiselessly to her side, nodding, smiling and smoothing down the bed sheets and tucking the corners in, envelope-style.

"I want to get out of here. I'm fine, really," said Gemma trying to lift her leg to get out of the claustrophobic room.

I just have to swing it over the side of the bed, she pondered. *Why was it not working*? She tried to lift her right arm. *Maybe it needs a helping hand* she thought to herself. Try again. No change.

Gemma couldn't move a muscle, not one single muscle. She tried again and again with all her might but it didn't matter how hard she persevered. She could not move. Worrying still there was no pain.

She heard the nurse address her gently. What was she saying? Gemma wished she had taken Arabic lessons but her job as a reporter with the Emirates Chronicle was full-on and she had been too pre-occupied to study.

"Gemma?" she heard a male voice call her name with a thick middle-eastern accent. Gemma looked to her left and saw a small, plump, dark-skinned bald man wearing square gold-rimmed glasses perched on the end of his nose. "How are you feeling?" the man asked, while squinting at the notes on his clipboard near the foot of the bed.

"I'm Dr Fariq, you've had a lucky escape," he added flicking over the notes on the grey steel clipboard.

"What do you mean escape?" replied Gemma, struggling to interpret what he had just said.

"The accident... Do you remember it? You were in a microlight accident near the racecourse in the desert," he asked moving closer towards the side of the pristinely-made bed.

As she wracked her mind to recall the incident, Dr Fariq knew it was normal for patients who had had a traumatic experience to block it from their memory, noticing how, although her hair was dirty and tattered, she was attractive.

"Gemma, I know it's hard for you to accept but the accident left your body badly damaged. You're lucky to be alive. You were unconscious for quite a while and if it wasn't for your companion and the quick response by the emergency services, well ..."

Gemma's brows furrowed as she began to search her memory banks to the time of the microlight trip ... she could see the birds, pink feathers, hitting the ground and hearing the sound of a horse whinnying in the distance.

"Abdul... What about Abdul?" Gemma cried.

"Don't worry. He escaped virtually unscathed, broken ribs and concussion but he will be fine. Abdul is my good friend and we have you in a private room under an assumed name for your security. Please do not worry," replied Dr Fariq.

Gemma breathed a heavy sigh of relief.

"I'm afraid I have to tell you that we have carried out extensive tests and the prognosis is not good," said Dr Fariq.

"Go on, what do you mean?" Gemma asked raising her eyebrows in surprise.

"We can't confirm it for definite, as yet, but the damage to your spinal cord may be considerable. I'm sorry. I'm afraid it is unlikely that you will not be able to walk again," he said lowering his gaze.

"No, it can't be true. You've got it all wrong. I've got an important meeting to go to," Gemma cried feeling afraid and confused, the tears welling up inside. Every breath she took was a challenge.

"The immobility you are experiencing is necessary. Even the smallest movement can have devastating consequences," he said quietly.

"There must be something you can do?" she pleaded, desperate for hope.

"No, Gemma; an operation would not solve your condition as the nerve damage is too severe. It could do more harm than good. I'm sorry not to be able to tell you something more positive. Believe me, we are doing everything possible. Rest now and I will return to check up on you," he said turning to walk out of the room. He hated breaking bad news to a patient, especially one as young as her.

Gripped by shock and disbelief, Gemma felt like exploding like a raging bull but realised she couldn't. A range of emotions flowed through her veins and she found extremely difficult to grasp the enormity of the doctor's words. *How did she feel*?

She had lost everything ... her career, her life as she knew it and now her mobility. Her world would never be the same again. The only part of her she could control was her mind.

She felt tears well up in her sad green eyes and one drop run from her right eye and down towards her ear. She daren't think about the months that lay ahead, wanting to be left on her own to lick her wounds and take in and digest the enormity of the situation.

Glancing at her bedside table her eyes lingered over the framed picture of her in the hills back home. Dumyat was reportedly a sacred hill where an ancient tribe once worshipped their god, legend had it. They and others fiercely fought the Romans for their freedom. It was a special place she would return to while thinking things out, especially after her parents' disappearance.

Gemma recalled walking with guide Duncan in the hills there and finding the smooth, clear crystal in the Wharry Burn. It made her feel safe and secure and she thought briefly about the strange vision of the Maeatae warrior Ethine and Cinoid.

"Where is my crystal, where is it?" Gemma said out loud. "Nurse, nurse!" she shouted. Several minutes later the nurse appeared. "Where is my leather pouch?" she asked anxiously. The nurse bent down and pulled open one of the white drawers of the bedside table, searched about inside with her hand and lifted out a brown leather pouch. Gemma's furrowed brow immediately relaxed.

"There it is," she said. "Could you ... could you put it around my neck please?" she asked urgently. The nurse tied the pouch around Gemma's smooth neck now almost obscured by a bulky brace. Gemma thought back to the time she last saw her crystal. The memories were coming back to her now, though a bit hazily. She was with Prince Abdul in his silver Aston Martin en route to the luxurious hotel when she realised she had forgotten to put her leather pouch containing the crystal back on, after showering.

She had telephoned Sharon at the flat they shared in Downtown Dubai and asked her to bring the leather pouch to the hotel. Then, in the secret library, Aalan told her she was the chosen one to return the crystal to the cave. She wondered how she had it now, as it was not in her possession when they leapt off the top of the building?

It was all coming back to her. Looking out of the window and up into the clear blue sky, her lovely green eyes filled with tears, streaming down her pale cheeks, Gemma looked at the fluffy white clouds forming the shape of a snowy mountain and drifted off to sleep thinking about her parents.

Gemma had been bitten by the journalism bug thanks to her mother Yasmin, who told her stories of her assignments as a foreign correspondent with among others - The Washington Post - the newsroom and what happened there, deadlines, excitement and thrills of her mother covering the big exclusive stories and the huge smiles on her face as she animatedly recounted the events and places mesmerised the young girl. From that time on it was all Gemma had wanted to do.

Brazilian-born Yasmin was on assignment in Egypt when she had met Gemma's archaeologist father, James, who was working on an important dig for the National Geographical Society. They had fallen in love and when Yasmin found out she was pregnant with Gemma, they had married and moved to James' home near Kilmartin, on the west coast of Scotland.

Growing up, Gemma saw little of her father as he was often travelling to digs all over the world and Gemma couldn't wait for him to return home with his tales of amazing and wonderful discoveries of artefacts and Viking treasure hordes discovered in far flung lands.

When Gemma was in her teens her father had the opportunity to take part in an important archaeological dig in South America. Yasmin, now a freelance journalist, was accompanying her husband to cover the story.

"But why do you both have to go?" cried Gemma after they broke the news to her.

"It is very important to my work Gemma," said James. "I want someone to report on what we find and it must be someone I trust and that is your mother," he said gently realising how big the wrench was going to be for his daughter whom he doted on. He knew Gemma worshipped her mother and was in awe of her journalistic career.

Brushing a strand of white blonde hair away from her face, James said: "We will be back before you know it. Gran will take care of you and going to Edinburgh will be a big opportunity for you to discover city life."

Gemma loved them both dearly and was dreading the thought of being alone. They had driven to Edinburgh from Kilmartin to drop off Gemma at James' mother's house in Leith before leaving for the airport to fly to Brazil.

As they drew up in front of the large Victorian-style house, Gemma saw her grandmother on the doorstep waving and smiling. She was small, slightly built with auburn hair, the energy of a woman half her age and full of Scottish charm and hospitality.

Walking down the five steps to greet her family she embraced all three and said: "Come away in with you. Let's have tea. I've some freshly baked shortbread and I want to hear all the news before you go," she said linking arms with Yasmin and Gemma, while James followed behind realising how lucky he was to have such a close family who cared so much for each other.

The dig was going to be a tricky one. James had been waiting on a permit for months for the excursion to Brazil. Finally, after cutting through red tape and using his contacts, it had come through and he couldn't wait to get there.

When the time came for her parents to leave, James and Yasmin embraced Gemma in turn and together and Yasmin said to her: "Look to the skies. When you see the sun and the moon and all those pretty stars, know that we will be looking at them too and will be thinking of you and longing for the time we will be reunited. Goodbye for now," they both said, hugging Gemma tightly there on the grey stone doorstep of the house.

James told her: "Open your atlas and find where we will be digging. Imagine yourself there and you will be with us in spirit."

As Gemma watched the black taxi cab pull away she could just make out her parents' faces looking out of the back window.

Two days' later her Gran, Mary, asked Gemma: "Fancy going up town for a bit of shopping and culture?" As she sat at the kitchen table Gemma sprinkled sugar over her porridge recalling her father remarking: 'Sugar is for Sassenachs; use the salt', but Gemma couldn't abide the tart taste and carried on using sugar.

"Sure, if you think I can stand it!" replied Gemma.

"We'll get the bus and go up the Royal Mile. It's going to be busy as the festival is on but it will also be a lot of fun too," said Mary, trying to cheer up her granddaughter.

The pair left the house and walked out of the garden before Mary bolted the white gate behind them. She looked to her right and spotted the maroon double-decker bus coming towards them.

"Quick, Gemma, we'll have to make a run for it. You go ahead and I'll catch you up at the bus stop," she said quickening her step as she watched the young girl sprint off ahead.

As the bus pulled over at the stop, the door opened and Gemma grabbed the steel pole inside.

"Come on Grandma," Gemma yelled before stepping inside. Once they were both aboard and had paid the driver the fare they sat downstairs right at the back of the bus and heaved a sigh of relief.

"So Gemma, what would you like to see?" asked her Gran looking at the passengers and wondering where they were going.

"I'd like to go to the museum," replied Gemma.

"Right, the museum it is," replied Mary looking over at the Scott Monument in Princes Street as the bus travelled over the Bridges heading for the Royal Mile, with the majestic Edinburgh Castle poised on top of the craggy rock on their right.

As the bus pulled over at the stop Gemma and her Gran stepped out of the vehicle and onto the pavement which was crammed with tourists and colourful street entertainers playing music, singing and dancing during the Festival Fringe.

Walking along the street, actors thrust leaflets into their hands urging them to come along to the performances. The crowds were now becoming so thick the pair could hardly move. Taking Gemma's hand, Mary moved across the cobbled road and into a quieter side street.

"My goodness, I was beginning to feel quite claustrophobic. Let's go to the museum and see if they have any special exhibitions on," suggested Mary.

Inside the light, spacious modern building they looked for a sign pointing towards the ancient Scottish section and wandered into the designated area. A small square box in the shape of a little church caught Gemma's eye. It had intricately carved copper and square circles on the sides and a sloping roof. Gemma read the notice: 'Brechbannoch Monymusk Reliquary.'

"It is believed to have contained a finger-bone of St Columba," said Mary. "Do you know who he was?" she asked.

"Yes, the patron saint of Scotland," Gemma replied eagerly, remembering enjoying history lessons at school and her father's vast knowledge of archaeology. "It was made by the monks of Iona," said Gemma.

"Yes. Very good! Can you keep a secret?" asked Mary.

Intrigued, Gemma replied: "Of course."

"Good, what I am about to tell you has been passed down through the generations of MacDonalds - the Lords of the Isles – and we are a proud clan.

"Yes, Gran but what is the secret?" urged Gemma, eager to know more.

Her Gran replied: "It is said that the reliquary did not contain the finger-bone of St Columba but housed a crystal instead, a crystal with very special powers."

"Powers... What kind of powers?" asked Gemma, becoming more fascinated as the story was retold. When Mary spoke she did so in conspiratorial tones, as if inviting her into a secret cabal.

"The crystal travelled through time, healing animals and people with its magical powers. It guided sailors through troubled waters and gave great strength to warriors in battle.

"It is believed that an Egyptian princess brought the crystal to Scotland, after fleeing her land which was conquered by the Romans. She sought safe haven with an ancient tribe which lived in the hills in Stirling centuries ago. Her name was Scota or Scotia," said Mary.

"What happened to the crystal Gran?" asked Gemma, urgently.

"Legend has it the crystal, in the Reliquary, was hidden inside an abbey on the west coast of Scotland and kept safe by the monks. It is said that when the

Knights Templar were forced to flee France from persecution, King Robert the Bruce of Scotland gave them safe passage through Ireland and eventually to the west coast of Scotland," Mary replied.

Gemma thought back to her conversations with her father about the warrior knights, who reportedly existed and were created to escort pilgrims travelling in the Holy Land. "They were reputed to be pious men and great warriors," her father told her. "They had beards but were forbidden to cut them and were sworn to chastity, poverty and obedience and if they were captured they could not ask for mercy or ransom themselves.

"They fought to the death. When they came to Scotland Robert the Bruce gave them safe haven and in return they help trained his men in guerrilla warfare and tactics; learned from the Moors in the Holy Land in preparation for the Battle for Scotland, which they knew one day would surely come. In 1314, at Bannockburn, they took on the might of Edward's Army. It was a great victory for Scotland over the English and a testimony to the military prowess of their leader, Robert," said Mary proudly.

Gemma recalled her father telling her about the events leading up to Bannockburn.

"I can't find anything in my history books which say that the Knights fought at the Battle of Bannockburn, father?" she had asked.

"Yes, I know, Gemma, it is my belief that they did. They certainly influenced it and the eight years of campaigning, leading up to Bannockburn. The Scots were winning and when the English foot soldiers recognised another force joining the engagement on the Scots side. There has been much discussion on whoever they may have been. Many scholars think it was the 'Sma' folk' a grouping of supporters, pages and some others who turned up too late for the battle.

"I suspect that such a force, however, would not have struck fear into one of the greatest military armies in Europe. In any case, this force must have been of considerable more importance as its advancement caused the English to flee, believing the day was lost. Yet, only years later, did the Scots under Bruce and the English ratify a treaty. If only the Scots had captured King Edward as he made his way to Stirling Castle this would have ended the war almost immediately, Edward's high ransom would have been all-deciding."

"Gemma?" said Mary. "You were miles away."

"Yes I was thinking about my father and the Knights Templar," she said.

"I know. He was so passionate about his discoveries and theories on history. I was telling you about the crystal," she said noticing a drinking cup in one of the glass cases to the side of Gemma.

"Do you know what this is Gemma?" asked Mary.

"No," Gemma replied.

"It's the Maplewood Bute or Bannatyne mazer - Robert the Bruce's drinking cup. On the central boss is a lion representing Bruce, with six plaques surrounding the lion all with the coats-of-arms of his loyal supporters and was passed from guest to guest during feasting. Look, Gemma, inside the cup, it's our clan crest," said Mary.

Gemma peered inside the mazer. "Which one is it Gran?" she asked.

"The one with the boat and sails, it's the MacDonald clan crest, my dear," replied Gran.

Several days later Gemma was playing in the garden with her Gran's black and white collie dog, Trixie, who loved to fetch and catch the red and white striped ball. It didn't matter how many times Gemma threw the ball, Trixie never got tired of retrieving it and Gemma's arm was beginning to ache.

"Enough, Trixie, let's have a rest and a drink." The pair sat down on the warm grass and Gemma's thoughts moved to her parents. She hadn't heard from them for a while but that was not unusual because of their remote location in Brazil. The last time she spoke to her father a few days ago he was excited at the excavation.

"Gemma, how are you? Mum and I miss you so much," he had said during the short telephone conversation.

"I miss you both too. When are you coming home?" she asked.

"We have made a fantastic discovery so we will be away longer than we expected. It is so exciting," he said.

Gemma's heart sank but then asked: "What have you found?" asked Gemma, though her mind dwelled on the thought of not seeing her parents sooner.

"I can't say over the phone but I'll send you a picture," he said faltering.

"Dad, Dad!" cried Gemma as the line went dead. Later, while checking her email, Gemma opened one from her dad. It was a picture of what looked like a smooth grey round piece of stone with white striations and the message: *Gemma, don't show this to anyone. Stay safe. We'll be in touch when we can.*

Puzzled, Gemma scanned and copied the picture to a removable disc and wondered where she could put it for safe keeping, before popping it into her black handbag. A few days later Gemma was in the garden with Trixie when she heard her name being called. It was her Gran.

"There you are," said her Gran. Kneeling down on the grass beside Gemma,

Mary said: "I'm afraid I have some bad news," she said taking her granddaughter's hand in her own. Gemma looked into her Gran's pale blue eyes, blotchy and red from crying.

"Gran, what is it?" Asked Gemma.

"Your parents ... they ... she faltered, bursting into tears. "Oh, I don't know how to say it. Gemma; your parents are missing."

Gemma stared ahead, the shock hitting her heart which felt like it had been burst wide open. "That can't be," she said. "What do you mean missing?"

"As you know they were working on the excavation and it seems there was an accident. An underground chamber collapsed. I just received the call from the British Consulate in Brazil that it is likely they were buried," said her Gran wiping away her tears with a white cotton handkerchief with a bluebell motif sewn in the four corners. It's strange what you remember in times of great stress or sorrow.

Gemma burst into tears and covered her face, sobbing uncontrollably while her Gran held her tightly.

Present Day Back in Jaball Hospital

Gemma awoke with a start, the pictures of her parents' faces fresh in her mind and she felt engulfed in a cloud of deep sadness. Not knowing what had happened to them had always left a sense of emptiness and sadness she couldn't explain to anyone. Her Gran had tried and tried to find out what had happened but the distance and translation difficulties wore her down over the years and ultimately led to her death. Is it true you can die of a broken heart?

The enormity of the doctor's words had stunned Gemma. A possible future began to sink-in the longer she lay there. And, over time, her initial reaction of disbelief led to anger that this could have happened to her. Acceptance was a long way off. One day just seemed to merge with the next. Time had no meaning and the routine was driving her mad ... the same things day in and day out. She felt like screaming but thought better of it. She then remembered Duncan telling her there may be days like this.

Dr Fariq uttered words of encouragement that she was doing much better and to continue with the physio-therapy - torture Gemma called it. The effort to make even the smallest movement took all her strength and courage and left her completely drained of all energy.

"Your visitor has been quite insistent. He's been here repeatedly and we have had to turn him away," said the nurse, patting down the sides of her white cotton sheets. "Will you at least talk to him even on the telephone?" she asked looking down at Gemma and smiling gently.

"I can't. I just can't let Abdul see me like this. It's better this way, really it is. Look at me, I'm crippled. I'm useless," she said, her voice beginning to falter as she turned her head away from the nurse to look out of the window, the same view day after day and night after night.

"If you are sure ..." replied the nurse walking out of the room. *Such a waste of a young life,* she thought silently to herself. Gemma's thoughts turned to her busy frantic days in the newsroom and the energy they exuded. You never knew what was going to happen from one day to the next. It was exhausting and exhilarating in the same breath. Gemma loved every moment of it.

It was, anyway until the accident - the day her world fell apart. She was paralysed and broken. She had been stripped bare emotionally, raw and vulnerable. For the first time in her life she was reliant on others. Gemma had always been independent, paid her own share all the time and she liked it that way. But now the tide had turned and relying on other people to do every little thing for her was degrading and humiliating, she felt.

"Right now, where's the action?" said a strong Scots female voice and Gemma recognised it straight away and, for the first time since her accident, managed a smile. Her PI pal Sharon had fantastic bluff and bluster but the stealth of a fox when she was on a mission. Gemma loved to sit back and hear all about her escapades with clients.

It was fascinating to hear her recount her adventures and stories. Some were funny and sometimes shocking - heck, the stories Gemma could write if it wasn't for that damn client confidentiality clause. Sharon was a big character, larger-than-life, both loud and colourful but a true friend and it was great to see her.

"Hmm, hope they are looking after you okay here, and if not you know I'll sort it out," said Sharon planting her Versace handbag beside Gemma.

She rummaged inside and plucked a square black box out of the bag which smelled of expensive leather and it reminded her of their girlie trips to the knock-off shop in Dubai's backstreets where they would often spend hours shopping in designer handbag heaven.

"How are you feeling today?" asked Sharon,. then, realising it was the wrong choice of word.

She was about to apologise when Gemma said: "It's okay, a Freudian slip."

"Here you are, a wee something to cheer you up." said Sharon about to hand Gemma the box and then realising that she wasn't able to grasp it let alone open it.

"Here, let me," said Sharon lifting the lid up with her beautifully red, manicured square fingers.

"Your nails are fantastic!" said Gemma, looking at them enviously before looking at her wretched broken ones."

"So, what do you think?" asked Sharon showing Gemma the box. Sharon picked out the glass square and read the words surrounded with Diamonte. It was truly exquisite. It read: 'No dream is ever big enough'.

Dreams, thought Gemma, *I have plenty of them and it's the only time I can fantasize and escape this wretched hell of an existence.*

"Abdul has been asking for you. Why won't you see him?" asked Sharon.

"Look, there's no way I'm letting him see me like this. What would he want with a cripple?" replied Gemma.

Sharon replied: "Maybe he wants to say 'sorry'?" She studied Gemma carefully. Then she decided to change the subject. "What did the doctors say?" asked Sharon.

Turning her head to look at her friend, Gemma said: "The doctors have told me the damage to my spine is so severe they still think it can't be repaired."

"Doctors, they aren't always right. I know you are going to get better," replied Sharon.

"I don't mean to sound ungrateful," said Gemma. The Doctor and nurses are very nice."

Sharon said: "Abdul contacted me to let me know where you are. I've been sneaking around and watching over my shoulder for so long I'm getting a stiff neck!"

"Thanks for everything ... Gemma said, sleepily. Sharon took her cue. As she left the room, Gemma closed her eyes feeling the soothing effect of the leather pouch around her neck. She wished she could touch it and take her crystal out and hold it in her hand just for a moment but she knew it was impossible.

Moments later she drifted off .... She felt a warm sensation near her heart. She was lying on the ground and heard the sound of a horse whinnying. She shivered, remembering the sharp sound of automatic gunfire, pink and white feathers, a crashing noise and thud. Then silence.

Suddenly, she could hear the sound of hooves vibrating on the ground. It sounded some way off and she tried to work out which direction the sound was coming from. She tilted her head to one side hoping to gauge the distance. It must be Abdul and Dancer. I want it to be them. I don't want to be alone. She could see only darkness.

The sound of the thunder of hooves intensified.

"It's them. I know it is. Thank goodness they're here," she sighed. The noise was reaching a crescendo. Gemma heard the sound of loud snorting and felt heavy breathing on her face. Something didn't feel quite right and she could feel the hairs on the back of her neck begin to rise and her heartbeat quickening, her palms becoming warm and sweaty.

She looked up and there in front of her was the most magnificent animal she had ever seen - a statuesque bold white stallion. Its eyes were as blue as the deep ocean. The horse began pawing the ground with its hooves impatiently, before rearing up suddenly. It looked Gemma squarely in the eye and then sped off at full gallop. It was racing along the golden sand gathering pace, going faster and faster.

Gemma's heart began racing. She could feel her fingers and toes, then her arms and legs; she was running along the wide beach, the cool surf splashing against her legs. She was smiling, laughing; her body moving as one as she powered along the sand. The feeling of freedom and movement was quite incredible. She wanted it to last forever. Then she was being lifted off the ground, rising quickly through the air, feeling as light as a feather. Gemma looked down and saw the top of the white horse's head, its great wings flapping by her side. She clutched the horse's mane for fear of falling off, then realised she had perfect balance, going with the rocking motion of the galloping animal.

They were flying higher and higher through the fluffy white clouds - the feeling of freedom and being at one with the animal was euphoric and exhilarating beyond belief. All her fears disappeared.

She could walk ... fly ... She was on the top of the world.

Then Gemma could feel the horse begin to slow down and drop. *No, I want to go higher. Don't stop. I don't want to go down,* she wrestled with the thought. She was back on the beach, her steps quickly becoming like lead weights. She was sinking, sinking deeper into the quick sand, going under, suffocating, she struggled to breath.

Gemma woke up with a jolt. She was sweating profusely, matted strands of hair stuck to her face. She was desperately trying to draw breath. The beach, the white horse, she thought. I was flying and running free. I swear I was! It was then Gemma realised she was rooted to her bleak hospital bed once more. The chill of the air conditioning caused her hot sweat to cool. Her skin began to tighten as goose-bumps formed. The reality of her future had finally sunk in.

Days quickly became weeks and apart from television, which was on all the time with the sound muted, Gemma had only the occasional visitor. One day she saw a news report on the Dubai waterfront. She recognised the Burj-Al-Arab Hotel nearby. Although she could not hear the report, what she saw shocked her. There on the beach was a mass stranding of dolphins. Gemma looked at the pathetic sight and felt like she had been punched in the stomach. *They couldn't be the same ones that I met,* she reasoned? Then she knew and understood. *Of course they were*! The message she had struggled with for so long was so very clear: 'We cannot save ourselves, but we will save you.'

The next morning Dr Fariq was making his rounds. "So how are we today, Gemma?" he asked picking up her notes on the file at the end of the bed. Knowing that the hoist was looming and not a prospect she was looking forward to one little bit, Gemma steeled herself. She could feel her left leg twitch.

"I can feel sensations in my legs and hands, doc. I really can," said Gemma looking up at Dr Fariq who had moved over to Gemma's shoulder.

"That's great. Well done," he replied, knowing that it was commonplace in patients like Gemma to experience these feelings but it didn't mean she would walk again. Residual muscle memory or something similar she had been told. Gemma's mobile rang.

"Damn, I thought it had been on silent mode. I'm sure I told the nurse. I can't even answer the damn phone myself ..." she grimaced. At least her hated neck brace was off so she could now feel the air around her head.

Gemma's eyelids began to feel heavy as she felt like having a short nap. She pictured Abdul and their fun times together at the races, dining in the restaurant, surrounded by sharks and other exotic fish.

"Gemma!" she heard her name. "Gemma, wake-up…" She recognised the voice but didn't know if she was awake or dreaming. It was Abdul's. "Gemma, I have been so worried about you. Why wouldn't you let me see you?" he asked, faltering.

"I ... I ..." she stammered.

"Look, I don't care what you are like. It doesn't matter to me. Friends stand by each other no matter what." he said leaning over and touching her gnarled hand. "We're going to get through this, Gemma, together, whatever it takes," he said tenderly. "Don't you know it's who you are inside as a person that matters? It's important that we are there for each other, no matter what." said Abdul sitting by her side.

"After all we have been through I don't think I could have done it without you."

"I hope so," she replied. "I really do," she said.

"You are very brave," he replied.

Gemma stared him in the eyes. "What is this about you having me committed?" she asked.

Abdul smiled: "So Sharon has told you."

He began to recount the story of what happened immediately after the crash. "Moments after we hit the ground I recovered and released myself from the wreckage. I was shaken and definitely 'stirred' he quipped, but quickly realised that you had not moved. I released your seatbelt and gently, supporting your head and neck, carried you out of the wreckage and placed you on the ground away from the ruins of my beautiful aircraft! I then called my friend, Dr Frank Fariq for advice and help."

Abdul looked at Gemma's curious expression. "Oh, yes," he continued. "We were at university together and roomed together. When I called him he came straight to the crash site with a discrete vehicle and full medical help. It was important that we secure your person and care where no one would think of looking."

"So where am I?" Gemma asked.

Abdul smiled and said: "You are in a very private and secure isolation facility that is part of the Mental Health Centre, of Jaball Hospital. My friend Dr Frank Fariq, Sharon, myself and the nurse, Aisha, are the only ones who know you are here. The room has its own private access stairs and elevator and is tucked away on the roof at the very back of the Hospital. You have the best of care and Sharon and I will visit discretely to avoid discovery."

Gemma felt better about the doctor, but realizing how vulnerable she was, asked Abdul: "What about the nurse? Can we trust her?"

Abdul thought for a moment and said: "I hope so, she's family. Aisha is Dr Fariq's niece." Gemma visibly sighed.

Abdul didn't want to tell Gemma about his father but felt compelled to. Perhaps she should know, he reasoned.

"Gemma, I've been here as often as I could be. I have had other important things on my mind as well as you. It's about my father. He's had a heart attack," said Abdul.

"A *heart* attack, how?" Gemma repeated, though she wasn't sure why.

"Yes, it happened when he was on a state visit to India," said Abdul.

"How is he now?" asked Gemma deeply concerned.

"He is very weak and I am attending to matters of state until he fully recovers," replied Abdul.

"I'm so sorry," said Gemma sincerely.

Abdul said: "Thank you. I don't understand it as my father is fit and healthy for a man his age. He was signing some papers with the royal seal when it happened," he said twisting the royal ring on his finger. Gemma thought for a moment.

"Look I've got a hunch. Why don't we get my cousin Sparks to analyze the ring and see what he comes up with?" suggested Gemma.

"The device is on the table next to your bed. I just hope it is crash-proof," said Abdul.

Gemma replied: "I'm sure it will be despite the crash and the 'ducking' in the sea. Sparks doesn't do things by half measures. What about Aalan?" Gemma asked.

Abdul said: "He's well and worried about you. He also saw what happened."

"So you have been back? And he's good? That's a relief. I had concerns he might have been abducted too."

"He is fine and sends his regards and prayers."

Gemma cleared her throat politely: "Robson, wake up! Midnight ..." Said Gemma. A light shone beneath the pink tablet then the cover magically opened up.

"Sparks!" exclaimed Gemma. Moments later the cheeky, red-haired figure appeared as a five dimensional hologram.

Abdul was stunned. "I've never seen a tablet do that before or anything like it!"

"Greetings!" Sparks said. *Nobody* said 'greetings' anymore, thought Gemma. He continued: "I was sorry to hear about your accident, Gemma. Sharon told me and said you didn't want anyone to contact you so I haven't been in touch but I have been thinking about you," he said. *It was true,* thought Gemma. *Sparks could literally fix the world, but affairs closer to home were more difficult for him.* It was as if other people's pain hurt him.

"It's just that I didn't know how to cope with what has happened," replied Gemma.

Sparks said, "I have been monitoring your progress. The device gathers data about your vital signs sort of like a Fit Bit, but more complex."

"Sparks, can you do me a special favour and scan Abdul's father's ring?" She asked.

"What are you looking for?" replied Sparks.

"We don't know; it may give us a clue as to how my father suffered a heart attack. He was wearing this ring at the time," said Abdul.

Abdul removed the ring and Sparks directed him to place it on a portion of the screen and he scanned it with special sensors.

"Will be back as soon as, Cuz, cheery bye," he told both before disappearing from sight.

"I'm a bit tired now Abdul, you understand?" said Gemma her eyelids feeling heavy.

"Of course, we will speak soon Gemma," replied Abdul as he watched her drift off into sleep, thinking how courageous she was.

Gemma could feel the leather pouch cool and comforting against under her chin. She was thinking of Turkey.

Turkey Two Months Earlier

When she left Scotland Gemma stopped over in Turkey for a week's holiday, not knowing when she would next be able to take a break. Gemma spotted the tattoo bar in the corner of the plush hotel. Curious, she walked over for a closer look. When Gemma had finalized her arrangements for the move to Dubai, she thought a short break would be in order.

The man was covered from head to foot in dark blue tattoos. In fact, Gemma noticed that a number of the guests had 'body art' but she wasn't convinced about it.

"Don't worry. It's henna, so it will wash off in time," the man insisted.

"What the heck. Let's go for it. You only live once," thought Gemma turning to the tattoo artist who was flicking through a book of tattoos. Gemma turned the pages carefully but couldn't see anything she liked. Just as she was about to get up off the stool her eye caught a white statue of a horse with wings on the ornate dark brown carved wooden table, nearby.

"Pegasus, Winged Stallion. He was originally a black stallion but black is portrayed as evil so through time he became white," he smiled.

I wonder if that happens to people, too, Gemma thought. With wings to be able to fly to freedom, now that's appealing. Gemma nodded to the tattoo artist. "Small and delicate" and pointed to the top of her right arm.

"Peki," he replied and he began drawing the proud stallion and little did Gemma realize that her journey was also taking wings...

Afterwards, Gemma walked down to the golden beach scattered with pebbles.

"These damn stones keep getting in my sandals," she said to herself. Desperately lifting up one leg after another and furiously shaking out the small stones. "That's better, take them back beach!" she scoffed.

Gemma then began to pick up four other pebbles - each with their own unique look.

There's a yoga session starting soon, Gemma had learned and headed off to join in. *A great way to stretch and relax* she had thought. When she reached the beach and the Zen Garden she met about eight other holiday-makers who had the same idea. In the garden, after a deep breathing session, Gemma began chatting to the Yogi and a tall, blond German woman called Brigitte.

"Be careful of spiders," the Yogi had warned in his broken English. They and the others had smiled nervously not sure whether he was joking...

He was bare-chested and wearing rust-coloured Yogi pants. That was the only way to describe them. Turning to Gemma and Brigitte he pointed to a spot on his arm. They couldn't see anything but he was convinced there was a bite mark.

The Yogi's name was Khan. Gemma asked him what it meant in Turkish.

He replied: "Emperor." *Interesting,* thought Gemma. She asked him about the strange black and white circle in front of the Zen Garden.

In broken English he explained: "There is dark and light in everyone."

And Gemma knew which pebble she would give him when it came to say goodbye. He wanted the courage to be a musician and teach his own 'system' as he called it. It involved yoga and energy but it got lost in translation.

Giving him a hug and pressing the white and black pebble into his hand Gemma looked into his kind brown eyes.

"Dreams can come true if you believe," she said. He looked down at the pebble and then up at Gemma, tears welling up in his eyes.

"For inspire!" he said. And Gemma didn't correct him. She knew what he meant. He had given her inspiration but she didn't know for what yet but somehow knew it would become clear when the time was right.

It was also going to be hard saying goodbye to Brigitte. The smooth white pebble was the one she would give to her.

"I would love to go to India and learn more massage and yoga but it is expensive," Brig had confided in Gemma in very good English. She had her own beauty therapy business back home in Germany.

Placing the white pebble in Brig's hand, Gemma said: "For inspiration."

Brig didn't understand the word but completely got the sentiment. "*Dankeshoen,*" she replied.

Back in Jaball Hospital, Present Day

Gemma opened her eyes and saw Abdul sitting in a chair beside her bed. He had sat there for hours while Gemma slept.

"I wonder how Sparkie's getting on," said Gemma. She glanced to her device on the bedside. "Robson, Midnight! Call Sparks." and the pink lid lifted open to reveal Sparks. Sometimes he reminded her of a 'mad' professor in his laboratory.

"Hi Cuz," he said when he turned to her. How are you doing?

Gemma replied: "Oh, you know ... surviving. What about you? We have both been anxiously awaiting any developments."

"I was going to contact you to let you know our findings but I wanted to wait until you were with Abdul. Gemma could see Abdul frown, probably wondering how Sparks knew they were together. She put him out of his 'misery'.

She said: "Sparks monitors this device and my contacts. He probably has a GPS on all my contacts too," She explained. "Isn't that true? She asked Sparks.

"Of course not, he smiled, that would be illegal!" he replied, still grinning. I was double checking before informing you both of the result. You know how it is when you have to depend on others ..."

"Sparks," Gemma said, "You're stalling. Come out and say it," She insisted.

"Well, it was unexpected and very interesting. Very interesting! My tests reveal that the gold showed traces of poison."

"Poison?" Gemma and Abdul said in unison.

"Yes *Cerbera Odollam,* to be precise. It's known as 'The Suicide Tree' and the species of tree belongs to the same family as Oleander. It is also quite toxic to humans.I also found out that the tree's seeds have a toxin known as *Cerberin*. This compound can cause disruption of calcium in channels of the heart muscle," said Sparks.

"So what you are saying is that it can look like someone has had a heart attack? Asked Gemma. Gemma and Abdul looked at each other in disbelief.

"Yes, it can lead to an irregular heartbeat that is often fatal if the toxin is ingested in high enough quantities," replied Sparks. "And there's more. I believe it may be the same poison from the first sample you sent me earlier. It was more degraded but the chemical signature was very similar."

"You said ingested?" asked Abdul. "So someone has deliberately done this to my father!" he said, the colour draining from his tense face.

"It's the perfect murder weapon. All you had to do is crush the seeds and disguise them with spices in the food. The plant is found in the Indian state of Kerala," said Sparks.

"My father was in India on state business," said Abdul. "I must go and investigate this further. I will be back soon," he said to Gemma, as she watched him rise to leave.

"Is this ring of some significance to you and your father?" inquired Sparks.

Abdul turned and replied: "It is the royal signatory seal of our family and is only worn by the ruler of our Kingdom. Why do you ask?"

"It is also something else. Something we like to call e-v-i-d-e-n-c-e. I advise you to bag it and keep it safe. Oh yes, and make sure you wash your hands after!" And just like that he was gone.

Editor-in Chief's Office, Emirates Chronicle

Yvonne rang the number she had been given some time ago. She had never had to use it until now. She felt uneasy and hoped it would not be answered. The receiver picked up. After a small pause Yvonne asked: "Aquil?"

"Why are you calling me?" he demanded.

"Gemma has been missing for two weeks. Her friend Sharon has been in touch to say she has had an accident and cannot work," she bit her lip nervously.

"So you have not located her yet? Get your people out! Check the hospitals, Health Centres, anywhere she could be treated and do not call me again until you know her whereabouts," he demanded.

Yvonne said: "She could be in Qamar or Abu Dhabi?" hoping to spread the responsibility for her perceived failure.

"Leave Qamar and Abu Dhabi to me," he replied curtly and cut her off. Aquil was not known for small talk.

Yvonne put down her telephone receiver. She was perspiring. Keeping the discovery of oil in Jaball out of the media was one thing, but the stalking and intimidation of her employee because she was doing her job was another. She picked up the receiver again.

Jaball Administrative Building, Qamar

Ever since the accident Abdul had been busy. Still battered and sore he returned to Jaball to be at his father's side. It was his burden to take the responsibility of his father's office: the administration of Qamar. Once he arranged Gemma's treatment and safety he set about strengthening the protection of the King, his father. Abdul had speared his accusation and suspicion of involvement at his brother but the petulant and surly

Khalid had protested his innocence and denied any involvement. Abdul clearly needed more evidence.

The preceding days and nights had been demanding as Abdul had set about the business of state with real diligence. When at last he reduced the workload to a respectable level he ordered a meeting late one night - no exceptions.

As he strode into Jaball Government Administrative building he moved with energy and purpose. In the elevator he selected the top floor and fumed while he ascended. All his requests about his attempted assassination and father's poisoning had fallen on deaf ears. As the lift door opened he walked to the end of the corridor and opened the door leading to the conference room. In the centre of the room was a large oval wooden table and on one side of it stood four men he had ordered to attend. Good, thought Abdul his insistence had not been challenged. He noted they all stood together on the other side of the table, with him but not *for* him, he concluded.

"You may sit." Abdul said. Three of the men did so, except the one on Abdul's left, Aquil. Abdul sat opposite them.

Aquil started to speak: "Prince Abdul, despite this unusual and late hour we are here at your request and if I may, I would like to introduce those present?" he hissed.

He's *trying to control the narrative and proceedings* reasoned Abdul, *I'll make an example of him.*

"Sit down Aquil, he ordered, this isn't a parade and I made no such request. It was a command!"

Next to Aquil sat the Head of Qamar State Police, Commander Adnam Al-Souf, still in uniform. Next to him was a younger man also in uniform but his rank told Abdul he was a Deputy to Commander Al-Souf. The last in line opposite Abdul was Dr Ali Sharand, Head of Pathology at Jaball Hospital, who also served as Head Medical Examiner for the State.

Abdul asked: "There is only one man here I did not invite?" and locked eyes with the man.

The Commander, older and overweight, began to sweat despite the air conditioned room. "Prince Abdul, If I may?" Abdul nodded. "This is my Deputy, Sharif, who heads the Department of Criminal Investigations. I invited him to come here tonight as he has been directly involved with the events you mentioned in your notice, part of which I was very surprised to read."

Abdul took a deep breath. "Those 'events' you refer to Commander could have led to the conclusion of two thirds of this Royal Dynasty and I don't care if you turned up with the whole police force as long as they have the answers I seek."

Aquil interjected: "My Prince, no one is more distressed than we that such a terrible act of barbarism could have led to your untimely death. However, I think that the Commander, in his obscure way was referring to the King's illness ..." Abdul watched the Commander nod repeatedly.

"Illness?" roared Abdul. "My father was poisoned! Under your watch, I might add! The men looked at each other for explanation.

Aquil said: "But Prince Abdul, your father had a heart attack. It was a natural occurrence and no one was to blame. He is receiving the best medical care anyone can get and we all pray for his speedy recovery."

Dr Sharand spoke up: "Prince Abdul, I personally spoke to the doctors treating your father myself. They diagnosed cardiac arrest and have treated him and will continue to treat him accordingly. He is in the best care we can provide."

Abdul pressed on: "What caused his heart to fail? He was in good health and received six-monthly checkups in line with policy. Should any indication of deterioration or illness not have been evident then? I checked my father's medical record myself and had it professionally scrutinized. There was no evidence of heart disease or any other indicators that might lead to failure."

"I have read the King's medical record and it is as you say, but poison?" Dr Sharand replied.

Abdul put his elbows on the table and pressing his fingers together, stared at the doctor intently. It unnerved the man.

"Are there not poisons that can kill a man and make it appear that it was caused by a heart attack?" Abdul probed.

The doctor stared at Abdul wide-eyed as if he feared he was about to be accused of medical malpractice or worse.

"Your Highness we do not ... we have no reason to suspect that if someone is ill it has to be caused by foul play," the doctor replied. Abdul did not want to lose the impetus of his interrogation, because that is what he intended this meeting to be.

"This isn't someone! This is the Ruler of the Kingdom and you should always suspect!" Abdul calmed himself. "Did you do a toxicology screening test, Doctor? He asked.

The doctor conceded: "No, Your Highness, we did not."

"Then perhaps you can arrange it immediately, Abdul turned his head to the right, indicating the telephone on the wall. Then we can continue."

The doctor raised himself up and looked at Aquil, who nodded. Dr Sharand crossed the room to the telephone and made the call. Abdul watched the interaction with interest. *Now we know who pulls your chain,* he thought. Two minutes later, Dr Sharand rejoined the others at the table.

Abdul turned to the Commander and his Deputy. "What do we know of the man who tried to kill me?"

The Commander replied: "Literally nothing."

"How can that be?" said Abdul. "You've had him for several weeks."

The Commander puffed and looked at his Deputy.

"I am afraid to inform you that the man is dead, Your Highness, and that the opportunity to interrogate him was missed," said Deputy Sharif.

Abdul considered the latest information.

"When did he die and how?" he asked.

The Deputy continued: "After the attempt on your life mercifully failed, the detainee was transferred to Jaball by a Royal Security detachment who delivered him into the custody of Qamar State Police. A short time after, the preliminary paperwork submitted, it couldn't have been more than twenty to thirty minutes, the man was found dead in his cell. The custody officer was questioned and the Medical Examiner was called for.

Death was found to be by natural causes. He committed suicide."

"I asked how?" demanded Abdul.

Dr Sharand cleared his throat: "The subject killed himself by swallowing his tongue, Your Highness, verdict suicide."

Abdul thought for a moment. "That's all very convenient. But who was he, what made him try to kill me and what about the unanswered questions?" Abdul asked.

The Commander asked: "What unanswered questions, my Prince?"

Abdul stared into the man's soul with his dark eyes.

"The questions, that clearly, have never been asked! I told you I wanted to know everything when it became available and now I have to drag you all here at this late hour and beg you personally!"

Aquil seized his moment: "Prince Abdul, we did not seek to keep anything from you, we thought, I thought, that with your father's illness and the many matters you have had to deal with it was best not want to burden you with more. I deeply regret such a misunderstanding, please accept my profound apologies ..."

Aquil looked at the Commander and said: "Do you not have something for the Prince?"

Commander Al-Souf leaned under the table and picked up a briefcase and opened it. He removed a beige-coloured folder and slid it over the table to Abdul. Turning the folder he read the details on the front cover.

As he did so Commander Al-Souf said: "This is all we have gleaned from our investigation into the assassin, the dead assassin whose name is, was Farouk Mosin

Ramash. He was eighteen years old and lived with his mother and two young sisters in the Shael district of Jaball. Ramash was not a Qamar citizen, as he was born in Syria as was all his family."

"I see no mention of his father," said Abdul.

Deputy Sharif replied: "The father did not move here from Syria with the family. We contacted Syrian Police and border control agency dealing with immigration. Apparently Farouk's father was killed in a bombing raid there."

Abdul placed the folder on the table. He thought for a moment and commented: "He doesn't seem to fit the profile of a professional assassin. It says here he struggled to provide for his mother and young sisters, that's a hard thing for a young man to do. I doubt he had much money to spare, not enough to buy the weapon he tried to use to kill me?" Abdul read on; No mention of radicalization or political activity. '*Why leave your home country to avoid trouble only to create it here?*' he thought.

At last Abdul addressed the meeting: "It doesn't add up. I see nothing here to indicate malice or motivation. This file raises more questions than provides answers. What about the weapon, a Sig Sauer 9mm P225/226 pistol, unless I'm mistaken?"

Deputy Sharif replied: "Yes, Your Highness, you are correct. The weapon had five rounds of ammunition in the magazine and the serial number had been machined off the slide and barrel. Therefore, we cannot trace its origin. We have contacted the manufacturer but without the serial number ... DNA testing of the weapon produced only the profile of the assassin and fingerprints on the weapon consisted of only Ramash."

Abdul pondered this latest exchange and had an idea. "OK, we'll leave it there, for now..."

The attendees got up to leave, visibly relieved. As they each left in turn or together, Aquil bowed to Abdul in exaggerated expression of action, bordering on contempt. Abdul nodded and thought, *'What is going on inside that head of yours, I wonder?'*

Later that Evening

Travelling back to his residence Aquil replayed the meeting in his head and thought he had done well. The unsuccessful and inefficient assassin had been disposed of. The weapon led to nowhere and the players in the act, Commander Al-Souf and his Deputy had been cowed.

The Commander was not much of a problem, having such a 'sensitive' son. The threat of exposure and ruination of his career had been enough. The Deputy, Sharif was easier. An ambitious but talentless young man, he was made aware that he would never progress in his career unless he had help to do so.

Only one thing had caused Aquil concern. The poison they had used. He comforted himself in the knowledge that it should have been absorbed into the King's body by now and they would find no trace. If only that idiot boy had not failed Aquil would not have had to sit through the pointless meeting. He had better things to do.

Next Day, Shael District, Qamar

Aquil was not as thorough as he had thought. Abdul finally located the address in the file after some painstaking searching and headed to the rear of the run down sandstone building. There he climbed up a metal staircase to the top floor and apartment number seventeen. Knocking smartly, but politely he could hear footsteps and eventually the door opened and a little girl about the age of five stood in rags (they could hardly be called clothes).

"Hello! little one, is your mother home?" He asked in Egyptian Arabic. Seconds later, her mother appeared and Abdul asked: "Am I addressing the mother of Farouk Ramash?"

The woman nodded politely and said: "Farouk is not here at the moment, what has he been up to now?"

Abdul considered his response. "May I ask you where he might be?"

The woman smiled. "He is at work in his new job" she replied and added proudly; "He is working for King Aariz," she replied.

Abdul was tinged with sadness. He knew the woman and Farouk had been duped, and now he would never come home ever again.

"That's quite a responsible job, Abdul said. How did he ever win such a lofty position?"

The woman picked up the youngest child and sat her on her waist. She said: "Oh, he was recruited. They spotted him on the street and said he was just the type they were looking for..."

Abdul smiled at her gullibility and pressed her further. "Who were they?" he replied.

"Two men in a black sports utility vehicle, Farouk said. Another man was with them. Farouk said he was a senior staff member of the Royal Household."

Abdul recalled how persuasive Aquil could be.

He was interrupted when the woman asked him: "Is anything the matter? May I ask who you are ...?"

Abdul reassured the woman and added: "Don't worry, Mother, all will be well." But he knew it wouldn't. As he returned to his vehicle, he paused and looked around at the dilapidated housing. This was exactly the kind of thing that should not exist in this world today. He resolved to see the woman and her family were cared for.

Chapter Eight

After Three Weeks in Jaball Hospital

Gemma awoke to the bright yellowish rays of sunshine peeping through the white shutters of her hospital bedroom window, convinced she had feeling in her toes and fingers and she was eager to tell Dr Fariq. He would be doing his rounds soon.

She thought a lot about Abdul and the time she spent in the Zen Garden in Turkey doing yoga for the first time.

Gemma had enjoyed her long walks on the beach where she gathered a collection of pebbles from the rock pools and had found a light paper-thin brown object. She realised it was part of a turtle's shell. Gemma had read that the earliest known turtle dates back 220 million years and that their shells are developed from their ribs and acts like a shield. The turtle is one of the oldest reptile groups but they are still hunted.

Gemma had learned so much about many different subjects. She absorbed new information and was like a walking encyclopaedia and it helped when she was doing research for her stories. But for all her knowledge and experience she remained close to the land and everything in it.

She recalled the time they first met at his father's stables in Jaball. Gemma had been sent out by her news editor to do a story on King Aariz and he had pretended to be a stable boy and didn't reveal his true identity as a Prince until on board the 'Flying Palace'. She had wanted to be cross with him but it was difficult as he had a very disarming smile. It was hard not to forgive him.

After the interview with his father she had become good friends with Abdul who got on well with Sharon which was a bonus too. Abdul gave her a tour of the state explaining all about his culture and customs, where his people came from, their heritage and Gemma had loved every minute of it.

"So how are you this morning, Gemma?" asked Dr Fariq.

"Well Doc, I can honestly say that I can feel my toes and my fingers," she said proudly.

"Mmm that's very good, Gemma. You have physiotherapy later this morning at eleven," replied the doctor, checking her notes and considering her comments thought to himself that phantom feelings are common in cases like Gemma's.

"I will be back later," he said before shuffling out of the room.

Physiotherapy? Thought Gemma, it was torture, more like! It was such an effort and towards the end of the sessions she wanted to give up but something deep inside of her drove her on. *What was it? Who was she kidding*? Gemma never gave up on anything. She remembered her 'sessions' with Duncan and shuddered as she did so. Gemma would not be allowed to give up on anything until she decided not to do so herself. That was how he motivated her.

Gemma pushed through the pain barrier and came out the other side with a sense of achievement and empowerment. Mind over matter is a powerful thing her dad used to say, and he was right.

Gemma focussed. I'll think about the torture later. Right now I want to concentrate on being back home, how things were before and she closed her eyes and could almost hear the piercing sound of the screech of raptors, the rutting calls of the Red Deer and imagined being in the hills and glens of Scotland.

She saw the birds being carried upwards on thermal layers high above the mountaintops and the view was spectacular, the sharp eyes were able to spot its prey where they would then swoop with expert precision and impale the helpless, unsuspecting creature with their razor-like talons before soaring upwards with their prize to devour in a safe place.

How she wished she was back there now walking in the great countryside. Through glens, spotting herds of red deer, pine martins and even red squirrels in the forests - being close to nature gave her strength and purpose. She closed her eyes again and kept them shut.

The faint sound of a horse whinnying caught her attention. Gemma could hear the sound of hooves vibrating on the ground once more and hoped it was Midnight. She felt her heart swell and as she looked up ahead of her appeared Pegasus again.

It began pawing the ground impatiently before rearing up again and Gemma knew what to do. She jumped on its back and the pair sped off along the white sand going faster and faster until Pegasus took off and they were flying high through the powder blue sky.

Gemma's heart was racing and she looked below and curiously could see herself running along the wide beach, the cool surf washing against her striking legs. She was smiling, laughing, her body filled with life and vitality as she powered along the sand, the feeling of freedom and movement was incredible and she wanted it to last forever.

Flying through the white clouds, the great white wings flapping by her side, Gemma was about to clutch the silky white mane-like before but she instinctively knew now she wouldn't fall off. She had been here before and this time she felt no fear.

They were soaring high and all her fears and anxiety had disappeared. She looked up and saw an eagle flying high above them, soaring up into the sky and the blue nosed dolphins swimming along either side of Pegasus. She could do anything, be anything and it felt fantastic. They were whole and as one. Now she understood. *Animus*; her animal spirit had manifested itself to her.

Suddenly she opened her eyes, the visualisation of Pegasus still fresh in her mind. She had been sweating profusely and strands of her white blonde hair had stuck to her face. She had no idea how long she had been away.

Instinctively, she wanted to brush the hair away from her face as it felt uncomfortable and clammy. Looking down at her right hand she noticed how straight and even it was. Looking over to the left one it was the same.

No it can't be. They were gnarled and clenched. Slowly, ever so slowly she lifted her right hand up, turned it over and did the same with the other one. Reaching for her face she wiped the strands away and up and tucked them behind her ears, then lifting both her hands in front of her face, she stared at them in wonder.

Tiny tears of hope and joy began to well up in the corner of her eyes as she dared to wiggle her toes. Please, make them work, she said to herself. Gradually, her big toes began to move and the others followed.

She rotated her ankles and stretched her legs, taking her arms above her head for a full body stretch; bowing her head and moving it from side to side and up and down feeling the tendons creaking and straining, the blood flowing through her muscles again felt fantastic.

But dare I try to sit up? What happens if I can't? Gemma closed her eyes put her hands at either side of the bed and shuffled up the bed before turning around to her thick white pillows.

"I'm doing it. I'm really doing it," she laughed out loud, tears of elation and relief running down the side of her pale face. Gently taking the covers back she swung her legs over to the side, pushing herself off from the bed and stood up.

"Just one step, that's all, take it nice and slow," she said to herself gathering up all her strength and courage for the biggest moment of her entire life.

Pointing her foot gingerly at the light grey and white tiled floor she placed it down and then placed her other foot in front of it. Taking a succession of small baby steps, she suddenly felt light-headed and reached for a nearby chair before falling over and crashing onto the ground, knocking a table containing her medicines and pills flying and onto the floor.

Hearing the commotion, Aisha the nurse appeared at the door to see Gemma lying on her side. She quickly helped Gemma onto the bed again. After making sure Gemma was okay, she left to find the doctor, who returned a few moments later looking a little more than flustered after the nurse told him what had happened.

After examining Gemma, Dr Fariq said: "For the first time in my medical career I am speechless. No-one who has ever suffered such severe injuries to their spinal column has recovered. I just can't believe it." he said scratching his head and taking off his glasses, absent-mindedly rubbing them on the end of his white coat with his squat fingers.

"Don't get me wrong, I'm delighted at your remarkable recovery. It is a ... he didn't want to say the word. I need to understand this!"

"Can I go home?" asked Gemma, desperately eager to have a shower and get back to the flat and normality again.

"No! Not yet, young lady. We have to carry out tests. This really is an amazing event which I would like to study further and more important you still are very weak. You have been lying dormant for a not inconsiderable length of time and you need to work your muscles to regain their strength," he advised.

Gemma sighed heavily but she knew he was just being cautious.

"I'll come back later when you have had some rest after all the excitement." He left the room still scratching his head.

'There's no way I'm staying in here a minute longer than I have to,' she thought to herself.

Picking up her lilac 'Diamonte' covered mobile phone for the first time since before the crash, her voice activated the number.

"Sharon. It's me!" she said. "Look, you've got to come and get me out of this place pronto. I'll explain everything when I see you and can you bring me a change of clothes?" and ended the call. She then called Abdul.

Looking down at her pale, rough hands and broken fingernails, she realised how unimportant having them beautifully manicured and polished all the time was. I'm just so grateful to have them working again as she flexed her fingers for the first time in ages. I'll never be ungrateful again.

It was dusk and Gemma was ready and waiting to leave her room which she feared would become her prison cell. How often and long had she stared out of the same white framed window at the skyscrapers opposite and watch the sun rise and set ... the days blending into weeks ... until time or life lacked meaning.

An hour later, he appeared at the doorway. Sharon was already there. He was amazed to find Gemma sitting upright in bed wearing clothes.

"Okay, so what's this all about, Gemma?" asked Abdul, who watched in amazement as she threw the covers away from her legs, swinging them over the side of the bed before standing up. His jaw dropped and he stood speechless. A moment later he walked over to Gemma, embracing her shyly.

"It was the crystal. Its special powers healed me," she said laughing. "That was the past, this is the future." She smiled. "Right, let's get out of here now. We've got some unfinished business. We have to find the cave." she whispered, clutching her pink tablet and packing her scant belongings. "You lead the way," she said, following closely behind him and closing her 'prison cell' door behind her.

Secret Library, Dubai Three Days Earlier

Abdul made his way to the back entrance of the Burj-Al-Arab Hotel. This was where deliveries and staff frequented and yet he did not feel out of place. Dressed in a staff uniform provided by Aalan, Abdul had swapped vehicles and ditched his mobile to avoid tracking. He took the staff elevator to the secret library and was warmly greeted by Aalan, who seemed anxious. "Good to see you my friend, but I'm puzzled why you are here. You must know this area is under observation?"

Abdul nodded and said: "I had to speak to you personally. When we spoke about the crystal cave and the Valley of Lost Souls, I felt you had more to say?"

Aalan considered his question. "It is true," he responded. "I left out a very important part. It consisted of a warning. Abdul, the cave has been sought after by many people for many, many years. Does it not seem odd that none have found it or come forward to say so?"

"Go on," urged Abdul.

Aalan continued, "I believe some people have found it, indeed, believed themselves fortunate to have done so and have paid a heavy price."

"You mean with their lives?" asked Abdul.

"No," replied Aalan, "with their sanity! Let me explain." He took a deep breath and continued, "I believe the name 'Valley of Lost Souls' is no coincidence. I have heard stories of men found wandering in the mountains, completely mad and gibbering in senseless tongues."

"What could cause such a tragic effect and how would a person hope to combat such a peril?" Abdul asked.

"It is said the crystals amplify a person's true nature and perhaps to a stage where they cannot recognize themselves. The good in a person will be enhanced and a bad person's nature will be enhanced too. By our true nature shall we stand or fall in relation to the power of the crystals," he continued.

History, thought Abdul, considering his own, as he felt this was what Aalan was referring to. "You've mentioned crystals, plural, twice. He said. Can you be more specific regarding history?"

"The crystals in the world are very powerful and mysterious things. Did you think there was only one?" asked Aalan.

Abdul felt the question was rhetorical and stayed silent.

"There have been many crystals through the eons of existence, perhaps before recorded time. If you had to send a messenger who carried vital information would you send only one? No, Abdul my friend, there have been many crystals and so far none have succeeded. How do I know this? I see the question in your eyes! I have perceived this fact for myself based on years of observation and gathering of information."

A message and a messenger, thought Abdul, trying to understand what this might mean.

Aalan said: "The world we live in, actually on, is a changing world indeed! It constantly moves and so do we all. Some say it has to move as it is a living breathing creature. How and why would such a being communicate to us if it had to? It would send out a message and wait for a reply! These 'messengers' have been with us for a very long time. Their influence shaped our history, as they surely have influenced the bearers for all the wrong reasons and perhaps now we have a slim chance to bring this quest to fruition."

Abdul evaluated this information. If the crystal is powerful and is the messenger, then he reasoned it must go back to the cave from where it came? He began to consider human history through the ages. The American Civil War, perhaps all wars. He had visions of Adolf Hitler, Joseph Stalin and other tyrants through history. What about Cain and Abel, too? The vast evil empires that held sway over millions of lives ... If what Aalan is saying is true, have we ever been in control of our own destinies?

Aalan said: "If you choose to do this thing my young friend, be prepared to risk all. The crystals do not play favourites. As for your young friend Gemma, I think her journey is linked to yours somehow. I cannot tell you where the cave is but the Valley is believed to be known. I shall reach out on your behalf.

Abdul thanked Aalan for his help and advice and left the way he had come, deep in thought. What was the message, he wondered?

Chapter Nine

Valley of Lost Souls

Gemma and Abdul had arranged for Nylah to meet them at a pre-arranged destination with supplies and mounts for their journey to the secret cave. When they arrived he was already there. Nylah had prepared Blossom and Dancer and saddle-bags full of food and water for the long journey into the mountains and valleys to locate the crystal cave based on the guidance provided by Aalan.

In addition to the two mounts they had three other horses serving as pack animals. In the desert there is scarce opportunity for water or food and that applied to the animals as well as the riders. Rather than risk running short Abdul had arranged provision of both. Nylah watched as the pair rode off into the cool night wishing he was going with them on the adventure but he would have to be patient and hoped his time would come.

There would be much danger ahead if they were heading to the Valley of Lost Souls. The journey would take three, maybe four days. His father had told him the stories of the *Pegi,* an ancient people who had worshipped in the crystal cave many centuries ago and Nylah wondered if he would ever see his friends again. He looked up into the night sky and prayed softly for their safe return.

Gemma was dressed in loose fitting, beige, cargo pants, a black vest and beige waistcoat. She had a warm jacket over the back of her saddle and wore ankle-length desert boots. To combat the heat she had on a light straw hat and a *Keffiyeh* or *Shemagh* scarf which covered her head and shoulders.

They made good time the first day, only exchanging brief commentary or observations that were necessary, until late in the day when they decided to make camp for the night. It had been blistering hot in the saddle and the searing heat seemed to bake them and the horses whenever they stopped. Abdul walked the mounts slowly while they cooled down, as Gemma began to unpack the other horses.

Abdul watched her as she did so, noting that she did not seem to show any physical problems after her long recovery; and in fact, Gemma seemed quite industrious. Before she could remove the twenty litre water carriers, Abdul suggested they swap chores and Gemma gratefully accepted. The 'camp' was a simple one. Abdul rigged what looked like two black-tented lean-tos' after checking the wind direction.

He dug a small pit in the sand and placed in some materials they had brought for a small fire. Over the top of this Abdul set a small metal tripod that had a chain hanging from the middle with a hook on the end.

Gemma watched Abdul place a pot on the hook after filling it with water and lit the fire. It seemed he had done this many times before and she thought Duncan would have appreciated his experience. Abdul turned to see Gemma watching him.

He said: "While that is heating up we will see to the horses; they always come first."

Gemma nodded and all the horses were given water and food. Once the horses were engaged in their fare, Abdul and Gemma checked all of them in turn for any problems. There seemed to be none and Abdul showed Gemma how to rig up a simple tether system using two poles and a line. They secured the horses loosely and turned to the camp barely feet away.

"We'll break out some food and perhaps coffee shortly but there is one thing I have to do first," he said.

From one of the packs he took out a grey-coloured metal container which had a spout on the end that was capped. Gemma watched Abdul remove the cap and walked around the perimeter of the camp about fifteen feet out pouring out a liquid as he did so. When he completed a full circle, he recapped the container and said to Gemma: "It's kerosene. The smell deters snakes and scorpions from crossing the circle. The nights in the desert are cold and they are attracted to heat. We don't want to wake up and discover any of them have snuggled up!"

Returning to the fire he decanted some of the now boiling water into a coffee press after adding coffee and poured two cups.

"This coffee is made from an Arabic bean and figs. It's quite aromatic."

Gemma took the cup and smelled the deep satisfying aroma, then had a sip.

"That's very tasty," she said and added, "Abdul you have been very quiet all day. What's on your mind?"

Abdul removed some dehydrated food from another of the packs and added dried apricots and sultanas. He added hot water and handed it to Gemma, who took the bowl and mixed in the ingredients.

As he prepared the same for himself he replied: "I was just thinking about something Aalan said to me when I went back to visit him..." He then briefed Gemma on what had passed between the two and admitted it was a lot to take in.

Gemma digested the information as she ate and drank. "You know, sometimes we are not meant to know everything. Sometimes it's just enough that we believe," she said.

He looked at Gemma and said: "Are you prepared to risk all? In light of what has happened, Gemma you nearly died!" This came out stronger than he had intended. "What if I cannot protect you?" He added.

Gemma thought for a moment and said: We'll watch out for each other ..." She could see he wasn't fully convinced.

Abdul said, "If you are finished, you should turn in. We have another long day ahead tomorrow. I'll clear up here and do the same."

Nodding, Gemma rose and went to the packs and removed two blankets. As she lay in her lean-to and gazed up at the night sky she suddenly became aware of her insignificance in the universe. The great desert sky, uncontaminated by artificial lights spread over the top of them and reminded Gemma how small we are all here on Earth. Billions of stars flickered in infinity. It was a masterful display of omnipotence. Gemma fell asleep wondering if they could all be alive.

She awoke when it was still dark and heard Abdul moving around. He had started to feed and water the horses and had restarted the small fire.

Gemma sat up and rubbing her eyes, she addressed his silhouette and said: "Why didn't you wake me?"

He looked at her and replied: "It's early yet. I was just trying to get things together, besides it was a hard day yesterday and we have another one ahead."

She stood up and felt a chill from the cold desert air.

"I'll pull my weight," she said indignantly.

He seemed nonplussed. "Check your boots before putting them on," he reminded her.

Taking down the lean-tos' Gemma wrapped them up for packing and along with the blankets. Then she took down the horse tether and gave Blossom a 'Good Morning' pat.

"A quick snack, some tea and then we'll be off," said Abdul. We should rest in the hottest part of the day, we will all need it."

Packed and ready to go Gemma took one last look around and noticed the stars quickly receding in the pale dawn light. *'Until tonight'*, she thought and then they were off.

Administration Building, Jaball, Qamar

Aquil stood by the window of his office in Jaball. It was night. His mobile buzzed and he turned and picked it up off the desk.

"Master, it is I, Akim. We have news of the fair-haired one."

"Go on," said Aquil, his pulse quickening.

"My men have been watching the stables as you requested and it was observed that Nylah the stable-hand began acting strangely. He packed three horses for a long trip, taking many supplies. But then more suspiciously, he saddled up Dancer and Blossom. It can only mean he plans to meet up with your brother, Abdul."

Aquil paused. "Tell me he did not discover that he was being watched? Did he see your men, Akim?" asked Aquil.

"No Master, they did place a small tracker in one of the pack horses. We are tracking him from a safe distance."

"Excellent work! Akim. You have done well. Tell me where is he heading?" Aquil pressed on.

"He is heading south, deep into the desert, Master," replied Akim.

"Contact the others and have them converge on the signal, but keep out of sight. We need to know their destination, only then can we know their true intentions. Do not lose that signal!" he ordered. Aquil then called Khalid with the news they had been waiting for.

The Desert of Jaball

The second day was much the same as the one before, Abdul pointing out the mountains in the distance, near the end of the day. At one time, Gemma had noticed a snake on the side of a nearby sand dune which seemed to have no sense of direction. She pointed it out to Abdul.

"It's a Sidewinder," he said, "very poisonous." Gemma studied the strange tracks it left as it soon disappeared over the dune.

The next evening, as they settled down to sleep, the stars reappeared in all their glory. Gemma felt and imagined they were her friends, there to watch over them. Gemma had sweated gallons that day. She was still acclimatizing to the desert. She smiled as she recalled Sharon on bringing up the subject when Gemma had first arrived in Dubai and commented on the heat.

Sharon had remarked in her best 'posh' accent: "My dear, horses sweat, men perspire and women simply *glow.*"

'*Well,* thought Gemma, *I've been glowing buckets today*!'

On the third day they both set off early as planned, but there was something different about Abdul. He seemed preoccupied and kept searching the horizon behind them.

"Do you see something, Abdul?" she had asked.

He shook his head, still searching. "No, that's what's bothering me."

Midway through the afternoon of the third day, Gemma could see the mountains shimmer in the baking heat and a mirage low on the horizon in the direction of the mountains gave the impression they were closer than they seemed. Resolutely, they ploughed on through the seemingly endless sands until hearing a shrill cry, Gemma looked up. Abdul noticed her distraction and did the same.

Shading his eyes, he said: "Egyptian Vulture."

"Why is it Egyptian?" Asked Gemma, as she watched the bird soar, using the thermals. Have we come that far?"

He smiled at her. "No, but they don't know they're Egyptian. The good news is they nest on high ground so we are close to the foothills." Two and-a-half hours later they had reached the foothills. They set up camp for the first time in the shade provided by a gully. The journey was harsh and tested their stamina to the limits.

Gemma was sore in places she never knew she had. Unless you ride regularly, you use muscles that have been dormant and they protest accordingly. She remembered her days hiking with Duncan and shuddered.

As they sat eating their evening meal Abdul said: "That's the easy bit over. We now have to go up in that same kind of heat. Are you up to the task?"

"Don't you worry about me," she responded. "I'll be right there."

He smiled and said, "I can see that. I'm also learning all kinds of things about the human spirit too."

They spent the time together enjoying the night and eventually, Gemma said: "Abdul, where are we going exactly?"

He thought for a moment. "Aalan wouldn't tell me, not exactly. But he did indicate where the Valley of Lost Souls is. When we go there tomorrow it should take about half a day."

"You mean he didn't know exactly where the cave is?" she said.

"That's the thing, he replied. I think he knew *exactly*, but would not tell me. It was odd, although I did not press him."

Gemma thought about Aalan, smiling, helpful and learned. *What Abdul told her was odd. But what did it mean, knowing and not just telling Abdul outright? Wouldn't that have made things simpler?* On that thought Gemma turned in for the night. Abdul seemed to linger. Gemma noticed that stars were obscured by a thin veil of cloud.

The next morning Gemma awoke with a startling feeling of positivity. Her body seemed to be getting used to the physical aspect of their travels. She strengthened her resolve and prepared for the day ahead. *Soon this will be over*, she told herself, *dig deep*. They set off as soon as they were ready and once more Abdul set the pace. The difference in energy required going up the mountains took its toll on the horses and they pecked frequently.

To Gemma, it appeared hotter, if such a thing was possible and Abdul led them up, across and down ridgelines in their search for the valley. After four hours they stopped.

"It's not that much further," said Abdul turning around watching Gemma who leaned forward onto Blossom, her head to one side of the horse's neck. Later they dismounted, as the going was steep and Gemma found herself puffing up the mountain. Walking alongside Apple Blossom she nuzzled into the mare's soft, silky white mane. The smell reminded Gemma of riding her own horse, Midnight, back home.

She was trailing about 200 yards behind Abdul, who was leading Dancer up the steep, rocky mountainous track.

"Come on; the view from the top is spectacular. You can see for miles and it will take your breath away, I promise," he said, striding on.

"Just what I need, less breath," panted Gemma struggling on, still clutching the mare's mane which was now becoming a bit knotted with sweat as they had been walking for what seemed like hours.

Before the journey Gemma had sent Sharon a quick, but brief text:

'Heading out with Abdul.
Will explain more later, Gx'.

When they stopped briefly to rest, Gemma asked: "Why does your brother want the crystal so badly?" Leaning against Blossom she listened.

"My mother died after giving birth to twins. My father was distraught with grief and never remarried. As I arrived first I am the ruling heir to the kingdom. Perhaps Khalid has never accepted that and will do anything he can to take the power away from me. Maybe he thinks if he has the crystal he will rule the Kingdom," replied Abdul.

Gemma and Abdul looked out over the harsh and seemingly barren land, considering this fact. They sat for a rest at the end of a valley that ran southwest to northeast. Abdul pointed to the other end.

"This is the Valley of the Lost Souls," he said. Gemma scanned the valley with her green eyes and noted that one side of the valley - the north - was covered in substantial vegetation. The south side was practically bare. Vegetation suggested the presence of water.

"What do you think?" She heard another male voice and turned around to see a tall man in a traditional long white flowing robe. "All this," he replied waving his outstretched arms around in a big wide circle.

"Truly, it is inspiring!" Gemma replied.

She observed the stranger. He was of average build with a long, wavy, salt and pepper sprinkled beard. By the lines on his deeply tanned face she guessed he was in his seventies but it was difficult to tell, as he radiated energy. There was something about him that intrigued her as she looked into the dark eyes that sparkled with mischief. He moved closer and just as she was about to ask who he was, Abdul appeared at her side.

"Do you need to be inspired?" the stranger asked. "What is it you desire?" he probed.

Noticing her inquisitive expression he again asked: "What is your heart's desire?" Gemma and Abdul looked at each other.

"Sometimes things that seem real are just an illusion," the old man said, sitting down on a nearby rock and clasping his weathered hands.

Gemma thought about what the man had said: *'What is your heart's desire?'* She had never thought about it before but after all she had been through, the crash, the hospital, being whole again, her deep friendships with Sharon and Abdul; her life had taken on new meaning.

What is my life's purpose? Gemma considered, privately to herself. Not so easy a question - not unless you have thought about it - but an important one nonetheless.

The old man looked thoughtfully, seemingly, into Gemma's soul and continued: "And you, my Prince, what is your desire?"

"How did you know I was a Prince?" asked Abdul, a little unnerved.

"There are two sides to a coin is there not? It is there to be seen by anyone with eyes," replied the old man.

Abdul pondered this reply for a moment and ventured: "My father's image is on the coinage of Qamar and no other," Abdul thought quickly and asked: "You can discern my father from the image but surely not detailed enough to identify his sons?" *And what did the stranger mean by 'two sides'? Could this man be in league with Aquil and my brother*?

The old man put his mind at rest: "You bear a small passing resemblance, it is true but you yourself volunteered the information of your status," the man smiled, got up and moved closer.

Now I will ask again, what is your hearts' desire? The day is late and the time is as yet, uncertain."

Abdul considered his response and said: "We are both looking for a cave." Best be reserved he thought.

The old man replied: "There are many caves in these mountains, too many to know in a single lifetime."

"Yes, but this one is a special cave but we are having a problem finding it," said Abdul. Perhaps he should be more cryptic. "A cave much celebrated in myth and legend that would perhaps, lead to much *reflection,*" Abdul added.

"You speak of the Crystal Cave, do you not?" The old man asked. They both nodded affirmatively.

"Do you know of it, I mean, where we can find it?" Gemma responded.

Now it was the old man's turn to be coy. "Crystals are mirrors and mirrors (he nodded to Abdul) reflect one's soul. Not everyone will like what they see in their heart. What is in your heart? Is my question and I will desire it answered."

"We do not wish to remove anything or seek riches," said Gemma. "We have come here to return that which rightfully belongs," Abdul nodded in agreement.

"Show me child; I know and have lived the legend. I saw your energy from up on the mountain where I dwell and came to speak with you out of curiosity of what I saw." The old man held out his hand.

Gemma looked toward Abdul and he nodded. Gemma then removed the leather pouch from around her neck and without opening it, placed it the open hand. The old man closed his eyes and Gemma and Abdul watched as he seemed be drifting into a trance-like state.

After a short time he smiled and opened his eyes. "It has been a long time my friend, welcome home!" He whispered under his breath. He handed back the pouch to Gemma, who placed it around her neck.

"You may not have realized it but this perfect wonder has been trying to return here through the ages. It has been guiding you, gently, as it has guided many others. Not all have chosen to listen or have understood.

You must go quickly. Time is running out. You must return the crystal," he said, standing up and leaning on his long wooden stick.

"You are not far from the cave. He pointed. Go northwards to the ridge, look for the Pegasus Constellation and you will find the cave," he added and started walking away along the mountain path.

How did he know I've got the crystal, pondered Gemma? She had so many questions unanswered. "Wait!" cried Gemma.

"Quick, let's go," said Abdul, striding over towards the horses who had ambled nearby. Abdul vaulted onto Dancer as Gemma grabbed Blossom's reins and mounted like a Cossack setting off at a gallop to find the crystal cave.

After a few hours the horses were tiring and Gemma was desperate for a drink, her throat felt like sandpaper. We've got to keep going, she resolved. Instinctively, Gemma looked up to the now darkening sky and saw the Pegasus Constellation.

"Abdul," she shouted. "Pegasus; it's Pegasus!"

Turning around he saw Gemma pointing her finger towards the sky. They both stopped their horses and looked up and saw the constellation, then the dunes, urging their horses on a little further, before pulling up at a rocky outcrop and dismounting. Taking out two goat-skin water carriers from his saddlebags hanging over the side of Dancer, Abdul walked over to a pool of water and bent down to fill them.

Looking up Gemma could see twinkling stars shining like jewels against the dark evening sky. Suddenly, the horses became agitated, their ears pricked forward, necks drawn up to full height so their veins were sticking out of their skin. They began prancing around and Gemma was finding it hard to hold onto them.

There was a faint humming noise which increased in intensity. Abdul saw a light in the sky, low on the horizon, which moved unlike the others. Then they heard the distant humming of the rotor blades. A black helicopter was fast approaching and a searchlight hanging under the chin of the flying machine turned on and illuminated the desert night. The light soon found them. The sound of gunfire echoed across the great desert mountains.

Gemma reached over and pulled the saddlebags off her horse before the animals suddenly reared up in fright and bolted off back the way they had come, receding into the darkness.

Reaching inside her bag Gemma plucked out her pink tablet, voice activated the machine, shouted for Robson to activate 5D after giving her password. Almost instantly, Gemma and Abdul's images were projected four hundred yards to the west drawing the gunfire away from them.

As she made her way over towards Abdul, Gemma slipped and plunged headfirst into the pool of water. An undercurrent was pulling her down deeper and deeper. She felt like she was going to drown and couldn't hold her breathe much longer, then suddenly she couldn't feel the water around her anymore. She was surprisingly sitting on hard ground, the water droplets trickling down the sides of her face.

She looked up and around her and was in awe at the colours and shapes of the giant crystals - deep pink, purple, orange, amber, green, shapes she had never even seen before. It was truly amazing. If I was a painter this would be a dream come true, she thought.

Where was Abdul? She could feel butterflies in her stomach and her palms beginning to sweat. *What on earth am I going to do*? Just then a figure appeared from nowhere and Gemma recognised the familiar figure in the long white robe. It was the old man. He walked over towards Gemma and sat down beside her. She looked at his face, the lines ingrained deep so deep they would stay in her mind forever.

Gemma said: "I saw you head down the mountain, I'm sure I did!"

The old man smiled knowingly and said to her: "There are many paths in life and they all lead to the same place. It is our destiny. Forgive me but the crystal had to bring you to this place, I had to be sure."

"We were simple people," he said clasping his big brown hands together and Gemma noticed he was wearing a gold ring, she recognized it as the same design as Aalan's, the library-record keeper, with a white Pegasus on it.

"We had nothing but each other and this huge task fell to us, how could we hope to succeed?" He noticed Gemma looking at the ring he wore.

"Ah Pegasus," he bent his head deep in thought. "You've seen this before I suspect? He has been called Protector of the Spirit, Guardian of the Soul and is a symbol of purity and justice. These special creatures matured into beasts that can mind speak," he said, his eyes glazing over.

"We have been waiting for the protector to return home and restore peace and harmony to our people and the land. Come, we must go a little further still," said the old man walking over to Gemma and holding out his hand inviting, her.

She felt his hand on her arm as she was guided through a kaleidoscopic array of hundreds, perhaps thousands of crystals of all shapes, colours and sizes and began negotiating her way through them.

"We are running out of time. I need to know if Abdul is okay," she said.

"Quickly," the old man urged reaching out with his old brown weathered hand. "This way," he said. He moved surprisingly fast for his age.

Gemma was mesmerised by the crystals' beauty: they were mind-blowing. However, her concentration was interrupted by a loud explosion from outside the cave.

"They're here. We don't have much time. Quickly, the crystal, we must put Pegasus back," insisted the old man forging ahead harder than ever.

The pair continued further into the heart of the cave before entering a small chamber. There, over by the wall was what looked like a simple stone bird table to Gemma and as she moved closer she could see it was filled with water. Then she remembered when she walking back home in the mountains of Scotland spotting an object which looked like the outline of a horse with wings but when she picked it out of the water it was an ordinary looking smooth white pebble.

She recalled lying in the hospital bed, paralysed. Her mind was the only muscle she could move and Gemma realized how the crystal had pulled her through, healing her back to health, bringing her here to the cave so she could return it to its home.

Suddenly, Gemma heard a loud shout and turned around to see the old man stumble and fall to the ground. Khalid was on top of him raining down blows. He then strode over towards Gemma.

"Give me the crystal," he demanded. "I will be the ruler!" he added menacingly, moving toward Gemma.

She could feel the hairs on the back of her neck rising and a sickening feeling in the pit of her stomach. *No, I'm not going to be afraid anymore,* she thought to herself. She got to her feet and remembered Duncan's words. She took up a boxing stance and raised her fists like she had been shown when learning the martial art of *Krav Maga.*

She felt her feet become light despite their earlier exertions. *Watch his hands* she told herself. *Watch the knife. He is telegraphing his attack. He is confident because he is bigger than me and because he has a weapon. That will be his downfall.*

Just then Khalid stepped closer towards her and waved his dagger in small figures of eight to intimidate.

"So let's finish that business now!" said a voice behind Gemma.

It was Abdul. "You are not fit to rule this country as the man you are," he said. With that, he leapt like a panther on top of his brother and the pair began grappling. During the fight with his brother, Khalid spotted Gemma out the corner of his eye. He then lunged towards Gemma who mustered up all her courage and strength and threw the crystal over towards the bird table and prayed. She heard the sound of a plop and breathed a sigh of relief.

"Not so fast," shouted Abdul pulling his brother back off Gemma. Just then a massive white beam of light began bubbling upwards and then shot up from the basin filling the entire cave.

The atmosphere was electric - the pink and purple crystals began vibrating, humming at first and then as they increased in crescendo, buzzing audibly. Then the yellows and oranges, blues and greens of the crystals in the cave, flickered and pulsated until the cave became a kaleidoscope of colours and sounds merging together like a symphony in an orchestra.

Not realising it, the brothers had stopped their struggle to witness the statuesque vision of an enormous white Pegasus stallion rearing up on its back legs in the pyramid-shaped cave towering over the trio below.

The powerful energy radiating from the winged horse was overpowering. Gemma could feel the white light being absorbed into her body and through her. She turned and looked over at Abdul and Khalid who were staring wide-eyed not quite believing what they were seeing - it was a feeling of being suspended in time.

Khalid could see his brother and him playing as young children in the palace grounds and wrestling with each other on the large lawns. He smiled and thought about how they grew up best friends but when Abdul left to go to university in England to study and, as number-two in Royal succession, he had to stay in Qamar.

The ruling Sheik's advisor Aquil, who wanted Khalid to become ruler so he could exert more influence on the weaker-natured Prince; tainted Abdul and Khalid's relationship so that it became bitter and acrimonious. When Abdul returned home after his studies their relationship was never the same.

Abdul could see Aquil whispering into Khalid's ear. Poisonous incantations meant to dissemble.

"You should be the heir to the Kingdom. Don't you know you were first born?" the advisor told Khalid.

"You lie! That's not true. Why do you say that?" argued Khalid in the palace library.

"I was there when you were born. I saw you emerge first, I swear," said the advisor.

"What proof do you have?" demanded the exasperated and unsettled Khalid.

"Come I will show you the records. Do not doubt me my Prince, as I have never doubted you," replied Aquil.

The advisor showed Khalid the fake document he had made up, showing he was born seconds ahead of Abdul and enraged with deceit he vowed to stop at nothing until he could seize what was rightfully his. It was the advisor's story about the Legend of the Pegasus Crystal and its powers which led Khalid to pursue it. Aquil told him the man that held the crystal would be all-powerful.

Just as Abdul was about to say something he saw Aquil switching the fake document for the real one in his father's study and putting the real one back in the safe after Khalid had left the room.

The brilliant white light was still beaming all around them as they stood rigid in the cave. As they remained transfixed their live drama played out before their eyes.

The next moment Gemma and Abdul saw Aquil inside a stately royal hotel suite speaking to the King and motioning him to sit down at the table. They watched as the advisor, with his back to the King, pick up a plate of food from the dresser, put his hand in his pocket and sprinkle something into the food before giving it a quick stir and putting it down in front of the unsuspecting King, who ate it. In true Arabian style they used their fingers.

When they had finished eating, they saw King Aariz take out the royal seal and just as he was about to stamp some papers, he collapsed in a heap on top of them. Abdul was stunned and for the moment forgot about Aquil. However, seconds later Abdul looked over to the bird table and saw Aquil reaching into the water for the crystal.

"You, you poisoned our father. You ... you tried to kill him!" Abdul roared at Aquil, jumping on top of him and pounding him to the ground.

Khalid attempted to grab his brother from behind but Abdul, when he drew back his elbow, hit Khalid hard in the chest. Gemma saw him fall into the well.

"The well, Abdul, the well!" she shouted to warn Abdul, who turned to see Khalid sink below the bubbling, swirling waters.

Seizing his chance, Aquil darted over to Gemma and picked up Khalid's discarded knife.

"Abdul, Help!" Abdul heard Gemma's cries and turned round to see Aquil holding the knife at Gemma's throat.

"My men will be here any minute and then I will be ruler of Qamar!" he said. "I was going to remove one Prince then why not two?" Abdul moved forward.

"Not one step closer or I will end her life," hissed Aquil, the reflection of the cold blade glinting in Abdul's face. He saw a reflection of the old man to the side and knew he had one chance to save Gemma.

Abdul looked up and shouted: "Look out Aquil, the roof is caving in!"

"I'm not falling for that old trick," Aquil shouted, stepping backwards with a terrified Gemma. Just then a lilac crystal dropped from the roof knocking Aquil unconscious.

Gemma moved over to Abdul who cradled her in his arms.

"It's over," he said.

"Not quite," said the old man. "Khalid's men are still outside. You must go now."

"What about the Khalid and Aquil?" Asked Abdul.

"Don't worry about them. I will take care of everything. Your quest is over. I will look after them. Your brother is not dead! His mind was poisoned by Aquil but the crystals will purge the evil from him. Dive into the pool and you will be safe. Go quickly my friends. When Pegasus rises all will be well," he said.

The pair could hear screaming and shouting just before they dived into the deep blue pool ... and then there was silence. When she surfaced Gemma could see

Abdul lying on the sandbank and swam over, getting out by his side.

"Abdul, are you alright?" she asked. There was only silence. She leant closer to hear if he was breathing but there was no noise. She began pumping his chest. Water spurted out of his mouth and he began spluttering.

"You had me worried there for a second," she said.

"I'm okay," Abdul replied. "I don't get a lot of swimming practice in the desert!"

"What does your name mean?" she casually remarked.

"Servant of the Protector," he replied, smiling broadly.

"That figures!" she said.

Close by they saw Nylah walking over with Dancer and Blossom.

"Where did you spring from?" Abdul inquired.

"I have been following you both." he said, handing the horses' reins to Abdul and Gemma.

"Thank you Nylah," they said in unison.

"Race you back to the stables. Loser mucks out!" shouted Gemma, putting her foot into the stirrup, swinging her leg over the saddle and heading off into the cold dawn followed closely by Abdul and Dancer, as Nylah watched them leave he mounted and followed.

As they headed back they had time to think of the future and discussed many things. Abdul, pleased to learn that his father would recover, but only after significant treatment and time, vowed to continue the service of his people. As for Gemma, it was back to the Chronicle...

After the Return from Qamar

Sitting in the comfortable cream leather high-backed chair in the Dubai newsroom, Gemma surveyed the cool, spacious office. Her article on the Royal Racing Dynasty and her incredible adventures with the crystal had earned her a promotion from Yvonne, the editor-in-chief. Gemma thought it a conciliatory gesture given her dealings with late Aquil.

Gemma stood up and walked over to the window. It was early morning and quiet just before sun-up with only the humming noise of a vacuum cleaner from across the hall disturbing the silence. The tall skyscraper-mirrored buildings dominated the skyline of this fascinating city.

Just as the sun rose, throwing out rays of fuchsia pink, orange and yellow, Gemma looked up into the sky and saw the fluffy white clouds being moulded into the shape of a giant Pegasus surrounded by a golden light. It was the most beautiful sight Gemma had ever seen. *What had the old man in the cave said? "When Pegasus rises all will be well,"* and she smiled.

Wullie's secret drinking had been discovered and Yvonne wanted to fire him but Gemma had persuaded her to retire him as her experiences changed the way she looked at people and challenging moments. Her telephone flashed up a text message:

'Hello sweetheart. Heard Abdul has been busy. No drilling for oil in Jaball!

Congrats. Catch up later. Sharon x.'

The sound of an incoming call tinkled from her device interrupted her thoughts about Sharon. She had hardly had time to draw breath since her adventures and couldn't wait to tell Sharon all about it in detail.

She answered the pink tablet watching the cloud form in the sky disappear.

"Gemma," said the voice she recognised as Sparks.

"Hi Buddy, how are you getting on?" he asked Gemma, as he appeared as a holograph.

"I'm cool. Congrats on your promo, I knew you would get it," he replied.

"Thanks for calling me back," Gemma responded.

"Remember that blood sample you sent me of yours to analyze on my new invention?" he said.

"Yes," replied Gemma.

"Well, I found out you and indirectly our family, have special blood.

"What do you mean 'special' Sparkie?"

"It turns out we are Rhesus Negative, a very rare type and people with that type of blood are believed to have heightened subconscious abilities."

"But I'm a MacDonald from the Highlands and my Gran told me I am descended from the Vikings," said Gemma, sitting down on the cream leather swing chair.

"You are linked to all these people, Gemma," explained Sparks "And more, much more."

"Is that why I had the visions, the crystal was trying to tell me who I really am?" she said, amazed at the revelation.

"No! Not quite. The crystal did have an effect, a notable one but that may not be all there is to it," replied

Sparks. He continued: "And I've got another piece of news for you," he grinned.

"I don't know if you can top that, Sparkie," said Gemma.

"Remember some of these amazing things happened when the crystal was not physically on you at the time? Well, it has been verified that your DNA has been altered, perhaps by the crystal.

"How *altered*?" asked Gemma.

Sparks replied: "Just that. Your DNA shows modific-ations perhaps caused by exposure to the crystal."

"That's fantastic, retorted Gemma, and hard to believe."

"How do you feel about another adventure?" he asked and before she could answer, said: "What do you know about dolphins?"

"*Dolphins*?" She replied, shaking her head. "Not a lot but I can find out." Then the image of her dolphin friends who rescued her after the base-jump, flashed through her mind - a rain forest, de-forestation, scorched earth, natives fleeing their primitive homes. "But why?" she asked.

"Because you're not going to believe what I have found ..." he said.

THE END

Gemma will return in the second book of the trilogy: 'Gemma and the Dolphin's Tale'.

Read the sneak preview on the following pages.

The Dolphin's Tale

The Amazon rainforest - Brazil

Gemma was tossed around and pushed down river by the heavy, swirling current. Trying to reach shore she punished her muscles in a bid to reach dry land. As she was swept around a bend 30 feet from shore she spotted her chance – a muddy bank covered in part with luminous sludge. Gasping for breath, she made one last mighty effort and swam towards it, the high pitched sounds of exotic birds and screeching monkeys echoing in the distance.

Reaching the brown, muddy haven she threw her body forward like a swimmer doing the front crawl. Just then Gemma was engulfed in a swarm of emerald green and black butterflies which swept upwards in a cloud into the blue sky.

Exhausted, her muscles aching with the monumental effort she has just made, Gemma managed to turn her mud-caked body and lie on one side, trying to recall how she had found herself here in the hot, oppressive jungle of the Amazon rainforest. The butterflies began to indignantly land on and around her as she gathered herself.

Beads of perspiration began trickling down the sides of Gemma's lightly tanned, heart-shaped face. A strange feeling squirmed in the pit of her stomach rising up through her nervous system, the small hairs of her arms and neck began standing on end. She had the distinct impression of being watched.

As she rolled over onto her front Gemma found herself staring into two large piercing green eyes only two feet away in the shadows of the forest. The huge black creature took a step closer, its large paw almost touching Gemma's face. As it edged forward, Gemma could almost feel its whiskers on her face. Her heart was racing - petrified - she couldn't scream. The creature took a deep breath as if inhaling her very life force and Gemma could only lie frozen to the spot, gripped with fear- this was it - it's over, she winced.

Then, as quietly as the creature had appeared, it turned around and slipped back into the dense foliage. Gemma breathed a heavy sigh of relief not quite believing what had just happened. She should be dead. The huge powerful cat - a ghost of the forest- had spared her, but why? What was the reason? It didn't make any sense.

After a few moments, she pulled herself up out of the mud and slowly rose to her feet. As she looked over towards the heavy undergrowth Gemma knew she would have to venture in- maybe there would be some friendly natives who could help her, though she had heard tales of tribes who still were hostile toward outsiders.

She reached for the side of her waist unclipping the leather holder and pulled out the knife. Looking at the gleaming blade, she thought: *'I have a chance. I have to make it out of here.'* Walking slowly into the forest it took a few seconds for her eyes to adjust to the darkness. There it was again - the big cat just feet away, looking over its left shoulder at Gemma with its large green eyes.

The connection was instant. The creature turned back around and began walking further into the dark jungle. And Gemma could only follow…

About the Author

Wendy A. Scott is an award-winning UK journalist with her own Scottish-based PR company..

While not working on Gemma MacDonald's next exciting adventure set in the Amazon rainforest of Brazil, 'The Dolphin's Tale' - the second book in The Crygem Series - she can be found happily mucking out stables and walking in the beautiful, majestic mountains of Scotland.

The Leith-born author is a former newspaper editor and reporter who lives in central Scotland with her partner and pets.

Milton Keynes UK
Ingram Content Group UK Ltd.
UKHW040248310823
427788UK00005B/200

9 781739 346904